NO TIME FOR STOPPING

I didn't get far, just about a block, when I heard my name, "Eddie!" I glanced over my shoulder, slowing but not stopping, because if you stopped and it was your enemy, your life could spill like soda right on the black asphalt, spill before you could touch your wound. I never ran with gangs, never kicked it with weasel-necked *vatos locos*, but you had to be careful, quick as a rabbit. Once a dude pointed you out in a 7-Eleven parking lot or some filthy gas station, there was no mercy, no time to explain that you were a father or a good son or an altar boy with combed hair.

ALSO BY GARY SOTO

Mercy on These Teenage Chimps

A Fire in My Hands

Accidental Love

Help Wanted: Stories

The Afterlife

Petty Crimes

Novio Boy: A Play

Canto familiar

Jesse

Local News

Pacific Crossing

Neighborhood Odes

Taking Sides

Baseball in April and Other Stories

gary soto

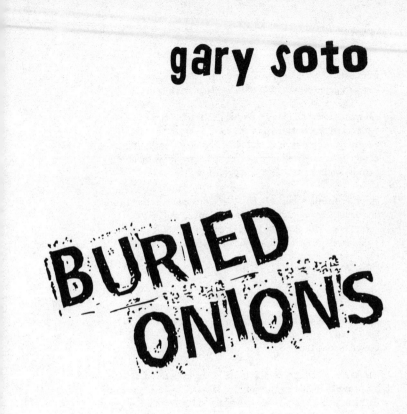

BURIED ONIONS

HARCOURT, INC.

Orlando Austin New York San Diego Toronto London

For information about permission to reproduce selections from
this book, write to trade.permissions@hmhco.com or to
Permissions, Houghton Mifflin Harcourt Publishing Company,
3 Park Avenue, 19th Floor, New York, New York 10016.

www.hmhco.com

First Harcourt paperback edition 2006

The Library of Congress has cataloged the hardcover as follows:
Soto, Gary.
Buried onions/Gary Soto.
p. cm.
Summary: When nineteen-year-old Eddie drops out of college,
he struggles to find a place for himself as a Mexican American
living in a violence-infested neighborhood of Fresno, California.
[1. Violence—Fiction. 2. Mexican Americans—Fiction.]
 I. Title.
PZ7.S7242Bu 1997
[Fic]—dc21   96-53112
ISBN-13: 978-0-15-201333-2   ISBN-10: 0-15-201333-4
ISBN-13: 978-0-15-206265-1 pb   ISBN-10: 0-15-206265-3 pb

Printed in the United States of America

DOC 20 19

4500698737

Text set in Trump Medieval
Designed by G. B. D. Smith

For the crew, cultural workers

Ray Camacho
Daniel Cano
Denise Chavez
Lilia Chavez
Sandra Cisneros
Deborah Escobedo
Eddie Estrada
Juan Felipe Herrera
Carol Lem
Yolanda Lopez
Ruben Martinez
Victor Martinez
José-Luis Orozco
José Padilla
Margarita Luna Robles
Eugene Rodriguez
Luis J. Rodriguez
Patricia Rodriguez
John Sierra
Simon Silva
Peter Tovar
Roberto Vargas
Helena Viramontes
& our late *carnal*
José Antonio Burciaga

CHAPTER 1

I knew the mortuary students would get good jobs because my cousin had died recently and my father and two uncles were dead, all of them now with arms like the arms of praying mantises, crooked and thin as whispers. My best friend from high school was also dead, his head having been caught like bulk laundry in the giant rollers of a steel foundry. It was his first good job, and his last. I pictured him with a head like a hatchet, and if I met him, say in heaven, or some dream that was close to heaven, I wouldn't know if I should say something first or let him speak the tinny words of someone whose head had been flattened by iron. "Juanito," I decided I'd say, cheerfully patting a bench to invite him to sit next to me, but looking the other way. "You remember when you stuck your finger in a bottle and couldn't get it out?"

I had gone to school with Juan since we were seven, and I knew his sister Belinda, now heavy with a baby, her second and possibly her last because her husband, Junior, was in Vacaville prison. She hadn't softened. She was a *chola* with wings of blue over each eye and a tear tattooed on her left cheek.

I thought about Juan while sitting at a wobbly metal table on the campus of City College. The mortuary students all had clean fingers and sat over coffees that I imagined cooled quicker than the coffee regular students drank. I figured that when they handled the bodies, the dead stole some of their heat, and later, when they climbed the steps of the dank basement, the students of that ghoulish business had to stand in the sun and quiver until the heat returned to their bodies.

The sun was climbing over the trees of City College and soon the black asphalt would shimmer with vapors. I had a theory about those vapors, which were not released by the sun's heat but by a huge onion buried under the city. This onion made us cry. Tears leapt from our eyelashes and stained our faces. Babies in strollers pinched up their faces and wailed for no reason. Perhaps as practice for the coming years. I thought about the giant onion, that remarkable bulb of sadness.

I returned to my apartment, which was in a part of Fresno where fences sagged and the paint blistered on houses. The swamp coolers squeaked like squirrels. Dogs pulled at chains, the clover leaf of their padded paws hardened by years of this kind of traction. Laundry wept from the lines, the faded flags of poor, ignorant, unemployable people. The old sat on porches, fanning themselves, stirring up that onion smell so that it moved up and down the block. Some guys, all of them Mexican like me, worked on their cars, and the young mothers stood on their front lawns, talking as they pushed their strollers back and forth a few inches. Still the babies cried, and their crying stirred up our frustration because we were like those strollers going back and forth, back and forth, getting nowhere.

2

For me, there wasn't much to do except eat and sleep, watch out for drive-bys, and pace myself through life. I had dropped out of City College, where I was taking classes in air-conditioning. I quit not long after my cousin, *mi primo*, Jesús got killed. He was at a club with Angel, his best friend and *carnal*, a blood brother. On that night he was exactly that, a blood brother, as Angel eased Jesús down to the sticky black-and-white tiled floor. My poor *primo*. He had died all because he told another guy that he had yellow shoes. They were in the rest room, at the sink I imagined, and my cousin was happy he had a job and a new woman, so happy that he wanted to talk. Jesús made the mistake of looking down at this guy's shoes and saying something. This guy pushed a dirty blade right into my cousin's clean heart. Or so I heard.

I tried not to think about Jesús, or Juan, or my father and uncles, all of them on their racks of black, black earth. But on those days when I saw the mortuary students huddled together, I couldn't help but think of them. I shook off those images and opened the door to my apartment. Roses flowered near the living-room window, sweetening the entrance. I had no more than a couch and two chairs, college books that I intended to resell, a bed and dresser, and family pictures angled so they almost looked at each other. I had a print of a ship riding the ocean, its sail full, going somewhere. It was fake art, the kind of thing you can pick up at a swap meet or get as a gift when you buy a gaudy red sofa from a Mexican furniture store.

The apartment was stuffy, hot. I turned on the swamp cooler, poured myself a glass of cold water from the refrigerator, and sat down with a sigh on the porch steps. I got up and checked the mail slot—nothing. Just a reddish rust stain on my fingertips. There never was anything, just junk mail and my gas and electric bill. Even my mother, who lived in Merced with her sister Gloria, who had hearing aids in both wrinkled ears, seldom wrote. I sipped my water while studying a red ant that was hauling a white speck, the bread of its living, pinched in its mouth. I chuckled. The ant was earning his keep.

"Keep running, little dude," I muttered. I told myself to keep a steady weight on my shoulders and to stay out of trouble and run a straight line—to stay away from the police and the rumblings of *vatos* who have nothing to do.

To get by, I stenciled address numbers on curbs. I had started doing this after an uncle from Los Angeles said it was good money. He didn't have to show me how. I bought spray cans of black and white paint and stencils, and usually worked the north part of Fresno, where there seemed to be more money. The lawns were deep and very green, and the flower beds saluted with all kinds of fistlike flowers. Most of the people were white, not Mexican. Most people there keep to themselves, not like here, in my area of southeast Fresno. We sit on front porches, our gaze following anyone who comes into our neighborhood. We know each other, marry each other, and hurt each other over small matters. Bad as things are, could be, we never commit suicide like the *gavachos* who can't take it. We live to the end, even if the end is when you are nineteen and crumbling on a dirty floor.

I drank my water, got up, and went inside to wash

my face. I stood before the mirror, raised my eyebrows so that three lines wiggled across my brow. I studied the lines, fissures that would deepen as I got older. I wasn't unusual, neither handsome nor ugly. My face was no different from the face of a brown person lucky enough to hold down a city job, like the person collecting litter along the freeway. I washed with scoops of cool water and for a second imagined that I was being washed over by a wave. I dried my face on a towel that was bright orange, just like the vest I would wear if I did hold down that city job.

I went to the garage to get my bike. My stuff—the paints and stencils, a piece of cardboard and a rag, a length of chain to lock my bike—was in the basket. I walked my bike to the front yard. The street was deserted. It was eleven o'clock and already everyone had retreated inside, either to get away from the heat or to tune into the Mexican soap operas—*telenovelas*. I straddled my bike and sat on the seat, not wanting to go. But I forced myself, pushed on the pedal, because like that red ant, I had to come home with my own crumbs. I rode the length of the driveway and into the street. The neighbor's dog, a German shepherd with a burnt-black nose, eyed me behind his milkish cataracts. He didn't bark. He just followed me with his eyes as if I were up to something interesting. But the business of painting curbs is just a matter of ringing doorbells and humbling yourself by asking the owner—old man or old lady—if they'd like you to put some numbers down. It's not high math, since the same numbers are used over and over. It's an easy job, the kind that shouldn't really exist. I mean, who ever gets so lost that he can't find his house? Even drunk, we stumble on home.

I didn't get far, just about a block, when I heard my name, "Eddie!" I glanced over my shoulder, slowing but not stopping, because if you stopped and it was your enemy, your life could spill like soda right on the black asphalt, spill before you could touch your wound. I never ran with gangs, never kicked it with weasel-necked *vatos locos*, but you had to be careful, quick as a rabbit. Once a dude pointed you out in a 7-Eleven parking lot or some filthy gas station, there was no mercy, no time to explain that you were a father or a good son or an altar boy with combed hair.

But it was Lupe, a guy from high school, another one of Jesús's friends, a homie who used to do glue and paint with my cousin in junior high. They used to trip together. I saw them, their mouths gold and their tongues red. They were just tripping, using up their time on earth.

"What's up?" I called. My chest heaved like a frog and the skulls of my knuckles popped through my skin as I gripped the handlebars. That's how tight I was. Lupe always brought trouble, or he was asking favors, mostly money. If you didn't have coins on you, he would hit you up for the sunflower seeds in your pocket.

Lupe crossed the street, looking both ways but not for traffic. He was looking for enemies; careful, always careful. We shook hands. The insides of his arms were blue with spidery tattoos, the sign of someone who is covering up the needle bites. "Angel wants to see you."

I looked away for a moment. The street was quiet,

disturbed only by the hiss of lawn sprinklers. Behind one of the doors, a baby was crying like a siren. I ran a thumb over the sweat that was already flowing from my brow. The sun was coin-bright and merciless. Not yet noon, and it was already tugging at the water inside us.

"I don't want to see him," I said, not facing Lupe fully, my head turned so that I could keep my eye on things.

"He wants to get the creep who did your cousin." Lupe looked down at the basket on my bike. At any other time he would have joked that only girls had baskets on their bikes. This was not the moment. "He can put the *cabrón* away on his ear. Shut his face forever."

"No way! I don't want to see Angel."

"Come on, Eddie." Lupe pleaded with out-stretched arms. "Angel needs your help. *¿Entiendes?*"

My *tía* Dolores, Jesús's mother, wanted me to settle matters, too. She wanted me to find the guy and ice him. But I didn't know how, really, how to find him or how to stick him once I did find him. I figured God would do that in time, God or some homie. But *Tía* kept at me, kept calling and leaving piles of home-made tortillas wrapped in dish towels on my steps. I ate the tortillas and folded up the dish towels, piling them in a closet. When she called, she sobbed and begged me to me to do something. I didn't answer the telephone these days.

"Where's Angel?" I asked after a moment of silence.

"The playground."

Homies hung out in twos and threes at Holmes

playground, mostly sitting in the shade, mostly staring at anyone who was not from there. The Hmongs knew to stay away, hanging at Romain, and the blacks had other places to go, mostly pulling their squeaky VWs in circles on the west side. Most whites didn't even consider coming by, or if they did, they were so Mexican in manner and dress that they were like us. The other whites—the ones who looked like they were models for Kmart shirts and Bermudas—they came at night to play baseball on our first-class diamonds. That's when the refs showed up, and the cops with their helmets blue as heaven.

"That's my message, homes. I ain't involved, really." Lupe told me to be cool and left in a light jog, pulling up his khakis as he skipped up over a curb. I watched him disappear into an alley. I thought that one day, maybe soon, he would enter that alley and never come out, just disappear in the vapors of another hot and vicious day.

I started over to Holmes playground and for a crazy moment I thought of that red ant with the white flake. "Keep straight," I told myself. "Don't mess up. Angel is a gangster."

I rode over to the playground, Club Med for those with time on their hands or those who had already done time as *pintos*. Noon glared like a handful of dimes. Sweat darkened my underarms. Sweat rolled under my T-shirt and bathed my feet inside my ragged shoes. By the time I pulled into the parking lot of Holmes playground I was the Ganges River, muddy and foul.

Angel was sitting alone on a green picnic table, his legs moving back and forth like an accordion. He was wearing his dark green Dickies, shorn at the knees, the kind of pants gardeners wear when they run a hose on a lawn. But Angel was no gardener. He lived at home, his eyes leveled to the television, a gun in his sock drawer, and a crucifix chained around his neck. When he needed money, he stole or ran a scam on someone.

Angel glared at me, hard. He was eighteen, a dropout, a guy who liked to get messed up, beer mostly and weed that wrapped its sweet smoke around his face and shoulders. But right then Angel gave off the scent of cologne and a breath mint. He threw his arms up and out. "¿Y qué, Eddie? Where you been?"

I straddled my bike, just looking at him, sizing him up. His hair was slicked back. He was lanky, not like Jesús or Lupe. Both of them were small but hard in the shoulders. Angel was vicious, sneaky. He had slammed baseball bats on other dudes, mostly Hmongs, and still managed to eat his tortillas and sleep well.

"Jesús is gone, homes," I said, wiggling the collar of my T-shirt, letting the steam come off me.

"Some dude iced mi carnal," Angel said. "He was your primo. He had a lot of respect for you."

Respect. That word got more people buried than the word love. One snide look, an arc of spit, a little shoulder bump, and it was "¿Y qué?" And you were laid low as a shadow.

"He's gone. You can't bring him back."

"Never said I was a doctor fix-it, homes," Angel said. His breath gave off more breath mint, but there was nothing sweet about his words. "I said let's get the dude so Jesús and him can be equal."

"Like equal time?"

"That's right, Eddie, like equal time." Angel slapped his knee and laughed the kind of laugh that wobbles your shoulder. His legs fanned in and out as he raised his face and winced at the sky. He laughed and then spit. "You always acted too good. Starting in school when you wore those white-boy *pantalones* and ending right now, homes." He shook his head and said, "Jesús talked about you all the time, how you lent him money and got him straight when he was messing up. You stood with the homeboy, helped with that weasel, Carlos. Jesús was your *carnal.*"

I bit back some words for Angel. *Pinche cabrón*, I thought. I got off my bike, leaned it against the tree that shaded the table, and climbed onto the table to sit next to him. We sat in silence. I pried a sliver of wood from the table and turned it over between my thumb and index finger, a thorn that I had known since I was a kid living on the swings and monkey bars. Noisy kids—all shiny brown, all thin with angles of bone poking beneath their skin—were there right now, swinging up high, laughing, and coming down low with straight faces. Laugh, straight face, laugh, straight face. It was life itself: One moment you were cracking up and the next moment you were dull-faced with nothing to do.

"I wish I had a soda," Angel remarked vaguely, his arms resting on his knees. He was watching three kids in flapping rubber thongs as they walked in a caravan, one in front of the other, crossing the just-watered baseball field with their towels pinched under their arms. They were going to splash in the two-foot pool. I had been one of those kids, and so had Angel, Jesús, and Lupe, all of us with spiky hair hardened by the chlorine in the water. All of us had crawled like mud-colored alligators in that shallow pool, crawled because it wasn't deep enough to rise to our belly buttons. We evolved from the swish of an alligator crawl to standing up, like dinosaurs, our claws ready to strike. Dinosaurs, I thought. That's who we are. Too old to run with gangs and too messed up to get good jobs. I smiled at this thought as I watched the kids in the thongs that spanked their heels with each step, the punishment of being *raza*.

"Me, too—I could do with a soda," I said to Angel. "A cream soda."

"That's a first-grade drink,"

"I guess I'm in first grade," I said. I flicked the thornlike sliver of wood and noticed a crumpled Chee·tos bag under the bench. It was another food I hadn't outgrown.

"I got to go to work, homes."

"What kinda job you got?" Angel asked, not nicely, pointing to the basket of paint, stencils, rags, and cardboard. His eyes were alive. He appeared nervous. "Paint cans! What, man, you ain't grown out of doing paint?"

"It's an easy job I got. And I don't sniff paint." I grabbed my mouth—that thing that got me into more trouble than good—with my fingers and pinched it so it flowered into a pucker of skin. "You see any paint there?"

Angel dropped his head, and I could see that he was looking at the Chee·tos bag. Without looking up, he muttered, "I think I know the dude."

I stared at Angel. He had a spider tattoo near his

throat, right under an artery that jumped with blood. I imagined that this spider fed night and day, fed on blood.

"I don't want to know," I said. "It won't help me."

"You scared?" He looked up.

"No. But Jesús is gone, and I can't do anything about it."

Angel lowered his head, spit, and didn't raise his eyes when I straddled my bike and said, "He's laid to rest, homes. Let him alone. Whoever iced *mi primo* . . . He'll die soon enough."

The north side of Fresno is mostly white, with a little brown here and a little black there. Koreans, too, and Vietnamese with boatloads of genuine smarts. It's strip malls, the flash of new car dealers with drooping flags, refrigerators lined up behind windows like robots, and off the main strip homes that are nicer, though their owners are plagued by the universal human worry: how to get money. After I left Angel that was my thought, too, now that I was down to nickels and dimes in my ashtray at home. I rode through a new subdivision, so new that the front yards were foxholes of moist earth. They were going to plant shrubs and trees and, in *mi loco* imagination, they were going to bury their onion. This way, they could cry out their sadness right on the front lawn. This way, they could say, "I got my onion now, go get yours." I smirked at this thought and wiped the sweat from my eyes.

I rode my bike, one hand on the handlebars, my head turning like a sprinkler, left, right, then left again. I was searching for a house to leap on. I found it right away. There was an older white guy in Bermuda shorts, fiddling with something in a cavernous garage. I glided my bike up his curb and stopped some distance from him. He didn't hear me. He fiddled with the thing in his garage and then fiddled with his ass.

"Good afternoon," I called, trying to be cheerful.

He slowly turned to me. His face was pink from the heat, and he was so old that shock or surprise no longer registered on his body. He walked slowly toward me in dry-legged bursts, the way a spider moves when you poke it with a pencil. I repeated, "Good afternoon" but added "sir" with a nice-boy lilt.

The man was maybe seventy-five. The pink in his face was the broken veins that belonged to a drinker, or a former drinker. You didn't get that way drinking soda or sugar-laced iced tea.

"Yeah?" he growled.

"I'm in your neighborhood today painting numbers on curbs."

"Say it again."

He was trying to tie it all together, what I meant by painting curbs and just where he was. Possibly who he was. His mind was squares and holes, and his eyes were watery from something he did to himself a long time ago, or even this morning—maybe a shot of bourbon from his TV tray. I pointed to the curb and shouted, "It would be nice for people to know where you lived."

"This is where I live."

"Yeah, that's it, sir. Where you live. You need some numbers on your curb—your address."

"The curb is good. Put it in with the house."

13

I knew this would be a hard sell and thought that maybe I should push away, let my bike glide down the curb and up the street until I was no bigger than a speck riding on the surface of his eyeballs. I peeked over his shoulder. I noticed that he was trying to move something on a small dolly. "You need help?" I asked with a jerk of my chin.

His eyes watered, and I couldn't help thinking that he had probably breathed in the onion of sadness all his life. Sure, he had a house, children perhaps. Sure, he had a wife and job that got him through. But his eyes were watering. He couldn't take any more. He had bought his final house, a new one with timed sprinklers, and he was going to drink from a glass on a TV tray from noon until dark.

"You need some help?" I repeated. I got off my bike and kicked the stand down. I wiggled the front of my T-shirt and remarked that it was a hot day.

"You need some work?"

I smiled. He'd finally caught on. "Yeah, anything you got. Weeds or digging." I eyed rolls of pink insulation stacked like tires and pointed: "I could roll that out, too."

"What?"

"The insulation."

He looked at it and waved it off gruffly. He said that it had already been done, and he was going to sell the leftover rolls.

"Any kind of work," I said. I moved into the shade of the garage. From there I could make out his wife running a hose on a newly planted bush in the backyard.

"I ain't got much," he said, and turned like a tin

soldier, slowly, letting his eyes fall on the dolly. It was nudged halfway under the air conditioner. "I'm trying to get this to the curb, do a little yard sale this afternoon. Belonged to my old house."

The man gave off a smell of booze. His hand was peppered with age marks and his skin looked as thin as a sheet of onion. You could shine a flashlight on one side and see the blood, bone, and veins under his skin.

"Say, you wouldn't want to buy it?" His eyes brightened.

"Listen," I said, embarrassed but desperate. "Listen, I'll move it for a dollar." I was tired of his not hearing, not catching what I was saying.

"You'll move it?"

"For a dollar."

He studied me through the lenses of his watery eyes. The squares and holes of his thinking were coming alive. He pulled tears from his eyes with a thumb. When he nodded his head, I quickly moved the air conditioner onto the cart and counted to myself, "one, two, three," then tilted it back. "Gimme some room," I said. I balanced the bulk of galvanized tin and Freon on the dolly and rolled it over the lawn to the curb. I let it down gently and looked at it for a moment, thinking that I had moved it too fast and that my effort, my strain and balance, didn't seem worth a dollar. But I figured my attention to the air conditioner's safety added to my service.

The man approached me. "Say, my wife is in the back." He pointed vaguely toward the roof of his house. But when he turned, spiderlike, she was standing in the mouth of the garage, with a toy shovel in her hand, the kind that comes with an Easter pail loaded with fake grass, jelly beans, and brightly colored plastic eggs.

"Larry, what are you doing?" she asked.

He straightened up and flapped one arm angrily. "I'm selling the goddamn air conditioner."

"No, you're not. We promised it to Barbara."

"Like hell."

That was my thought. I was standing in the sun, one hand on the dolly and the other hanging at my side like a dead eel. I wanted my dollar, and I wanted to leave. My bike was parked in the sun, and I feared that with this heat the spray paint cans might explode.

The woman approached in slow, wide steps, and suddenly the three of us were hunkering over the air conditioner. They argued over that thing, both blasting trumpets of hard-liquor breath. I moved away to look at the curb, sizing up the place where I might press my stencils and paint numbers. It gave me something to do until they finished.

"Sir, I got to go," I said finally. "Can I have my dollar?"

He looked at me, his eyes wet, and behind that wetness, an image of me as a speck of light on the back of his retinas. He didn't seem to know what I was asking.

"My dollar, sir."

His wife looked up at him. "What did you promise this boy?"

"He moved the air conditioner." His voice was an apology.

"It belongs to Barbara." The woman turned to me and boomed, "This man is an old fool."

Right then, head lowered, I got my bike and rolled it down the driveway, looking at neither of them. It was three o'clock and what I needed they had but wouldn't give up: money.

I did find work that afternoon, six houses nearly all in a row, all new with half-finished landscaping, all proud that they had numbers on their curbs. Kids hovered over me. Dogs poked their long snouts between my legs. I was a young man at work. I nearly cried over the attention. I drank two sodas and one iced tea, and then gratefully jotted down numbers for gardening work. I rode home in the early dusk, my paint-sprayed knuckles ridged with white and black, like the crossbones of a pirate flag. I was tired but happy. I had money in my pocket, and the joyful music of coins clapping like tambourines as I pedaled.

I parked my bike in the garage, locked the garage, and got a long drink from the garden hose before I slowly walked to my apartment. On the front porch, there was a gift of towel-wrapped tortillas from my aunt. I picked them up and pressed them to my chest, warm as a body. The telephone was ringing. It was my aunt and she wanted revenge, too, wanted me to put someone away for good in a grave. It wasn't bad enough that we had to live through the vapors of buried onions and poor jobs. We needed dying.

CHAPTER 2

You can pray and sometimes God listens. Other times he's far away in India or Africa or maybe close to home in Fresno, his body sprawled on the floor, glass all around because of a drive-by. Maybe the walls are ripped with the pucker blast of a semiautomatic and tables and chairs overturned, the recliner's cotton guts spilling out and a framed portrait of President Kennedy tilted at an angle. The prez is looking skyward as if asking, "What more?"

What do we make of God and all the *movidas* on this planet? What do we make of a good-hearted jokester like Juan, whose head was ironed out in those huge industrial rollers? He was doing exactly what he was told and what the Bible and his family asked of him: Get your ass out there on a straight line and work. I had to laugh at this. If hard work is the road to salvation, heaven must be packed with a lot of people from Fresno.

"Angel, you gangster," I whispered as I rocked my head no, no, no on my pillow. He was anything but an angel. I thought about how bad ass he was—he even stole the crucifix that hung from his neck. Sometimes when I saw him, kicking at the playground or Fashion Fair mall on the north side, he would rake the gold chain back and forth on his front teeth and our Savior would dangle like a Christmas ornament in front of his lips.

I thought about God and Angel while I lay in bed, my legs and arms twisted every which way like pipe cleaners. When the telephone rang, I jumped out of bed, but I didn't bother to answer it. I knew it was my aunt at her kitchen table, a cup of coffee and one sugar donut within reach of her palsied hand. I tiptoed across the cool floor into the kitchen and thought of her tortillas, three eaten last night and the others now hard as Frisbees. I made a sandwich with bologna the color of a brown, crippled shoe. I rained Fritos into a large paper bag, my favorite lunch when I was a boy in elementary school, and still my favorite.

One of the curbs I'd painted yesterday was for a man named Stiles. He promised me more work, digging a hole and doing some landscaping.

"I got a job," I sang to myself.

I hurried out of the house, munching a banana. I reached into my pocket and brought out the address on a piece of crumpled paper. "Mr. Stiles," I mumbled to myself and prayed. "My dear Savior Mr. Stiles, please come through." I pocketed the address and rode up the block, still cool with shadows, sprinklers already slapping their rationed water on dry lawns.

As I arrived, Mr. Stiles was drinking coffee and surveying his yard, which had a small bump he intended to smother with a tree, flowers, and ornamental rocks. He waved when I rode up. He was dressed in Levi's with the thighs worn pale and a plain white T-shirt.

"Morning, Eddie," he said.

"Good morning, Mr. Stiles," I greeted him, happy

that he had remembered my name. I got off my bike and moved it up the driveway into the shadow of the garage. I got a job, I thought to myself.

"Is this where you want that hole?" I pointed to the hill he had raised with a truckload of clean fill.

He walked over to the hill and stood on it, his shadow like a flagpole behind him. He threw back his head as he drained his coffee and then jumped up and down, smiling, puffs of dirt rising around his work boots. I knew he was imagining how his yard would bloom and his neighbors would stop to admire it. In mid-May it was a nice dream.

"I'm going to plant a birch," he said as he climbed down.

I asked him about the tree, and he said it was the kind of tree that grows in New England, especially along the shady twists and turns of babbling brooks. I couldn't imagine such a place. I couldn't imagine a place where the sun didn't gnaw at my eyes, gnaw with its bright hunger so that every other minute my pupils had to adjust themselves. I closed my eyes for a brief second and wondered what this tree was doing in Fresno. No rivers spun through our town, and it certainly didn't look like New England, though we did have one barren subdivision called Connecticut Meadows. I had to laugh at that because most of the people who lived there were Korean.

Mr. Stiles said to dig where he'd been standing. I climbed onto that little rise of earth, which I worried a hard rain might wash away down the street, yet another dream that got away. I stomped my shoe and asked, "Right here?"

"Exactly."

I got the shovel from the garage and went to work. I dug with fiery scoops because Mr. Stiles was watching me and I wanted him to know that I was dedicated to my job. I could keep going for a while, keep shoveling, because I had to make a living and I had read more than a hundred times the story about the little train that could. That was me, a train with empty boxcars but a caboose of problems. Mr. Stiles watched, and when he turned I slowed down just a little bit, because work is one thing and killing yourself is another.

Mr. Stiles disappeared into the garage and I slowed even more, my coals of eagerness burning down. I dug at an even pace, stopping to wipe the sweat on my sleeve.

While Mr. Stiles and I had been talking, had been outlining the plans for landscaping, a kid on a tricycle had been going up and down his driveway. Now he pedaled toward me, stopped, and asked what I was doing. A box of animal crackers was swinging from his handlebars.

"Putting in a birch tree," I told him. "Do you know what a birch tree is?"

The kid shook his head.

"It's a kind of tree that people in New England like. Do you know where New England is?"

The boy shook his head.

I told him about the brooks and birch trees. I told him that deer ate from birch trees and were so friendly that they let you pat their heads. I didn't know what I was talking about, but I was a regular Robert Frost. The talk of green leaves and water seemed to quench my thirst.

"I live there," he said, jabbing a finger at a house. Then he added, "It ain't nice for you to say *bitch*."

I looked at the kid with a plain, brown face like a paper bag. I told him, "I said *birch*, not the other word." I thought of cops in blue helmets. I thought I better take him seriously. I didn't want his mom complaining to Mr. Stiles.

The kid slipped an animal cracker into his mouth—a hippo, I thought. He looked at me. His eyes were blue and his nostrils were dark as the holes in a Tinkertoy. "*Bitch* is a dirty word, man." He squeaked away on his tricycle, his pudgy knees going up and down. I watched him ride three houses away, up his driveway, and into the garage.

I worked all morning, first on that mound where the birch would go and then in the backyard, where plum and apricot trees would stand. At one hole, while I was on my knees working at close quarters with a trowel, I discovered an onionlike bulb, maybe the source of all our weeping. I examined the bulb and knew it wasn't an onion, but I laughed to myself and said, "Mr. Onion, you're going to die." I slashed the bulb in two and it bled clear tears. I sniffed it. It didn't give off an onion smell, just an earthy vapor that reminded me of work and nothing more.

I slaved in the yard that day and the next day, too, mostly shoveling because the ground was hard and Mr. Stiles was in a hurry to get the landscape in before July. Mr. Stiles was a good person. Now and then he brought me glasses of iced tea or a soda. He fixed me and himself a sandwich, with a red plastic basket of potato chips.

On the third day when I arrived he was in his garage and looked disturbed, moody.

"Hello, Mr. Stiles," I said, thinking that what he needed was a greeting. I also thought maybe he had run out of work and didn't need me anymore—at the end of each day he had paid me thirty dollars. With this money I had loaded my cupboards with Top Ramen, cans of soup, jars of applesauce, and Jell-O boxes the colors of the Mexican flag. I was ready for life, ready to get down and shovel all the way to China, if the money was right.

"Eddie," he said calmly as he walked up to me, his head lowered. He gave off a smell of cologne and coffee. A red vein throbbed by his left eye. "Eddie, my neighbor said that you called him . . . a foul name."

I put my kickstand down, puzzled. I fanned the front of my T-shirt, cooling myself.

"The neighbor boy. His mother is upset with me."

I pictured the kid with animal crackers. Little punk, I thought, feeling that every hole I had dug had crumbled in and now I had to do everything over again. "I don't know what you mean, Mr. Stiles. I don't cuss, usually."

"She was very upset when she told me," Mr. Stiles said. "We're all trying to get along in this neighborhood."

"Sir, I told him I—you, I mean—was planting a birch." I stopped for a second, sweat from my five-mile ride and the moisture of my fear working together into one powerful potion. I wasn't sure if I should use the word. Then I did. "*Bitch*. That's what he heard. He got it all wrong, sir."

"Bitch?"

"That's right. I said you were planting a *birch* and he heard the other word."

Mr. Stiles stared at me. A chill blossomed on the back of my neck. I was scared in a large spooky way, because the kid on the tricycle might eventually become a cop.

Mr. Stiles kept me on, and I worked because I needed money and he needed me to get things done cheaply. Mr. Stiles and I went to the neighbor's house to explain the miscommunication. The woman was hard until I said about six or seven times that I had nephews and nieces and I was so much against cussing. The matter was settled while the little creep clung to his mother's pants.

I worked all day and all the next, feeling the sun's heat on my back. I worked with a sledgehammer, chipping up some already broken concrete Mr. Stiles was going to reset into a patio with Chinese lanterns.

On Thursday I set the broken concrete for Mr. Stiles, who had returned to being the straight-ahead, let's-get-it-done kind of dude that I first knew. He even listened to me as I told him about how I was studying air-conditioning, a lie that whipped from my tongue like a lizard's tail. I didn't say I had already dropped out of City College and was waiting for the moment to resell my textbooks, which were square as concrete pavings and almost as heavy. But I described my ambition with such certainty that I began to believe that one day I would be tightening bolts on rooftop air-conditioning units. I wanted him to know that I was going places, even if it was only to a gravel roof.

One day Mr. Stiles said, "I want you to take a run to the dump."

With sweat weeping off my brow, I jabbed the shovel into the ground where a fancy flower bed would go and let it stand like a spear. Dirt smothered my face.

"You do have your license, don't you?" he asked.

I patted my backside and crowed, "Sure do."

He had loaded his Toyota pickup with scraps of wood, chicken wire, chunks of red brick, paint cans, stiff brushes, three threadbare tires, and noodles of weeds. He handed me the keys and a twenty-dollar bill for dump fees.

"Get a receipt," he told me. His eyes were bluer than ever, and his cologne was a cool fragrance for a hot day.

"Sure will," I answered. "But you know the tires are going to cost."

Mr. Stiles nodded. He knew that recaps cost three bucks a tire to dump. He had calculated that and calculated the drive, the dump, and the drive back to his place—an hour and a half at most. After I had worked for him five days, he figured I was a solid dude on a straight line.

I had messed up a lot in high school, messed up on beer and sometimes glue. But now I wanted God to come down and straighten me out with his golden pliers. I wanted a job like other people had, wanted to shake off homies like Angel and Lupe and the gangsters at Holmes playground.

"Back in a flash," I said, almost saluting. I was happy to be trusted and happy to be doing anything other than letting my shovel rise and fall.

"Stop for a soda." He handed me a dollar's worth of quarters.

"Thanks," I said, rattling the coins cheerfully inside my cupped hand. "I won't be long."

I jumped into the truck. I peered into a rearview mirror greased with fingerprints and adjusted it. My hair was dusty. There was a stream of mud at the corners of my eyes, a mixture of dirt and sweat. I looked like I'd been crying mud, as if my insides were some black lagoon. I didn't bother to wipe my face.

I started to the dump. I bounced with the sway and clunk of the heavy load while I cranked up the radio, one hand on the wheel and the other tapping out the beat on my thigh. When I first got my license at seventeen, I cruised around Fresno in my mom's Dodge Swinger. That car had a radio and Fresno had one sweet oldies-but-goodies station, and what was better than driving in circles looking at girls? The car was ugly. We had to hold down the cracked speaker in the dash. Otherwise the songs sounded like someone playing "Good Vibrations" on a comb covered with waxed paper.

I drove down First Street, where Holmes playground was located. I smiled to myself and muttered, "Those slimeballs are going to trip when they see me."

I drove slowly by Holmes playground, craning my neck as I searched for Angel and other dudes. I didn't see any of my gangster friends. The place was empty as a cemetery, the grass a faraway deep green. I circled the playground, but there was no one. Just a woman with her baby, the hatchets of her dark eyebrows raised. I thought of honking the horn at her but kept my hands on the wheel, my knuckles white as bone.

"Stupid Angel," I muttered. "He's probably halfway inside someone's window." I pictured his legs kicking as he slid through the window. A lizard or weasel, a snake, even, with a rodent squirming in his mouth—that's who Angel was, a thieving creature.

I drove to the Orange Avenue Dump, where the American flag was raised high on a mountain of garbage, visible for miles.

"What you got there, young man?" the man in overalls asked from a small building that had the shape, size, and smell of an outhouse. He didn't bother to look at the back.

"Weeds and bricks and...," I started to say. I thought about lying about the tires and paint cans but decided to go halfway honest. I didn't mention the paint cans. "And three tires."

The man did his math on fingers pudgy as Farmer John sausages. "Three, six, nine, eight for dump. Seventeen dollars. City tax. Eighteen dollars and thirty-five cents."

I almost stood up in the cab of the truck as I reached into my pockets and brought out the twenty-dollar bill.

"I need a receipt."

The man eyed me with a tilted head, as if he was thinking, Now what is a Mexican kid like you going to do with a receipt? I knew that if I hadn't asked for one, he'd have pocketed some, or all, of the money, right there in front of the American flag.

"OK, boss." He grinned and punched a cash register that spit out a receipt.

I ignored his redneck, hillbilly smile and drove

down the slippery, bumpy trail of garbage, following signs that said: THIS WAY. Landlocked seagulls were partying on a ripped mattress, their beaks clattering against tin cans. A junkyard German shepherd lay stunned in the shadow of stacked tires, overtaken by this nightmare place he patrolled and called home.

In the late spring sun, the place stank of grass clippings and rotting garbage—chicken bones, half-chewed hamburgers, milk cartons, tuna cans. Everything that we put on our plates and then scrape off.

"*Fuchi*," I complained to no one. I had to pinch my nose closed and breathe through my mouth.

I found a place and emptied the load. I hurled off the bricks and tires. With a steel rake, I pitched the weeds. I shotput the paint cans and was ready to leave when I spotted a refrigerator, the kind that goes in a dorm room. It was sitting on a broken sofa.

"Sweet," I cooed as I walked like an astronaut over a spongy layer of ripe garbage. I opened the door of the refrigerator three times, and each time the door closed with a clean pucker like a kiss.

After I loaded up the refrigerator, I got the hell out of that mess, pulling up the long, slick hill with a few flies clinging to my shoulders like buddies. I waved at the dude in the office and pulled the Toyota toward Orange Avenue. If my truck had been wearing shoes, I would have stomped the stinky stuff off them. Instead, I peeled out. At the first stop sign I skidded, scraping some of the stink off the tires. I was on my way.

I drove back to the city limits, radio blaring and the wind whipping across my arm as it lay on the edge of the window. I was nervous for taking time out, but

I stopped off at the apartment to stash the refrigerator, the centerpiece for a yard sale. My neighbor—the woman in the other half of the duplex—had blocked the driveway with her ancient Buick. I parked the truck on the street and hurried toward my apartment.

"Dinosaur," I snarled at the car, spanking the fender with the flat of my palm. I snagged a quick glance through the window at my neighbor, Mrs. Rios. She was crowing with a friend. I imagined they were breaking powdery donuts into halves and dunking them in creamy coffees, locked in the communion of older women talking *chisme.*

I unlocked my apartment and staggered into an oven of heat that nearly blew me backward.

"Beat it," I said as I looked at one of the dump flies clinging to my shoulder, its belly weighted with honest-to-goodness garbage.

I got a drink of cold water from the refrigerator, changed my T-shirt, and washed my face, the dirt rolling off like eraser rubbings. I even brushed my teeth, thinking that bacteria from the dump might have floated there and settled down to ruin my health. I chugged more water and listened to my neighbor laughing about her two-week bingo streak at St. John's Church. She was a retired nurse who had once put me back together when I had gotten into a playground fight. I had taken a blow from a stick on the bridge of my nose and one on my ear, plus a couple of whacks to my back as I chased a dude with the brown, jagged crown of a broken beer bottle. She had patted the blood from me and cooed, *"Ay, Dios"* over and over.

When I left my apartment, I was skipping like a kid. I hurried to the front but almost dropped to my knees when I discovered that the Toyota truck was gone. In its place was a vapor that could have been heat or onion. I scanned the street, chest already heaving, and looked wildly about. "Damn! I was only gone a second!" I whispered. I ran down to the corner and looked left, then right. The Toyota was moving quickly down the street with my refrigerator in the back. I couldn't tell who was driving but the dude was Mexican, his brown arm on the edge of the window—he was already comfortable with his new machine. I pictured him adjusting the level of the radio and feeling for stuff in the glove compartment—Bic pens and pencils, a flashlight, electrical tape, fuses, and fistfuls of matches. I pictured the thief finding a plastic box of Tic Tacs and throwing them down his throat.

There was no way to catch the truck, no way to call back those few moments I stood in front of the bathroom mirror combing my hair. I pulled on my hair, yanked it until it was a black torch standing straight up. Hopeless air left my lungs as I screamed, "You stupid glue rag!"

I walked slowly back to the front yard of my apartment. I stood on the lawn, where a sparrow was in search of his wormy pay. I pushed my hands into my pockets and brought out the car keys on a plastic four-leaf clover.

"Yeah, right," I said to the clover.

The neighborhood was quiet, the swamp coolers spinning on the roofs, and somewhere down at the end of the block there was loud laughter from a television program. Two doors opened and shadowy figures showed themselves, not wanting to get involved but curious, because at least once a month someone drove off with one of our cars.

"Piece of shit," I said.

I didn't want to get involved, either. I wished I had just stuck with stenciling numbers on curbs and had not let my ambition for digging holes get to me. So much for ambition. So much for trying to run a straight line like ants.

I hurried back to my own apartment, where I hid in the doorway and my own cavernous shadows.

The early dusk was ribbed with a low-level bank of pinkish clouds. Two future gangster kids were whacking each other with plastic bats, a playful duel in the yard across from me.

I was drinking a beer, my third, and hiding in my backyard on this day when I had started off on my bicycle and ended up on my knees praying that Mr. Stiles would understand why I never returned. The two other beer cans lay crushed at my side. I was buzzed. I felt like a deflated inner tube hanging in a garage, black from depression, because I had done what people and the Bible told me to do: work. But that advice had failed me.

"Hey," I greeted a stray dog nosing the yellowish stand of weeds that ran along the fence. "What's happening?"

The dog turned its sadness to me, his nose as black as electrical tape, his tongue splotched gray and pink, his eyes watering as if he had been sniffing onions.

"Hey, you gangster dog!" I yelled. I clicked my

fingers and the dog, streetwise, hurried away on three good legs. His left hind leg was not touching the ground.

I felt empty. I liked Mr. Stiles and I liked his dream—an ornamental tree in the front yard and fruit trees in the back. How could I ever explain what happened, how I just stopped home to drop off a refrigerator, chug cold water, wash my face, and comb my hair so that I looked human? No use. I had lost my bike, and lost his faith, a too common Fresno story that would not break anyone's heart. Almost everyone I knew got their cars or trucks stolen. Either that or they were the ones doing the stealing.

I heard a car pull into the driveway. Shame, not fear, made me jump. My heart pumped. I thought it might be Mr. Stiles.

"Who is it?" I called.

I was relieved to hear the *click-click* of a woman's pumps, not the stomping of shitkickers.

"It's only me," my aunt Dolores said, Jesús's mother, a woman I had known since I was ruling my block on a bike with training wheels. I had become close to her after my father died and my mother started reading meters for Pacific Gas & Electric.

My heart slowed. I sat back down in my lawn chair when my aunt rounded the corner carrying a red towel that contained a stack of tortillas.

"How come you never answer your phone?" she asked, immediately starting in.

I got her a lawn chair.

"I'm never home."

"*¡Mentiroso!*"

"It's true," I said, my arms out as if asking for alms. "I've been busy."

My aunt looked at me. The roots of her hair were white, and she seemed tired, as if she had been ironing all day. She placed a hand on the back of the chair. She asked, "Why won't you help me, Eddie?"

"*Tía*," I said, standing behind my own chair. "It's insane. You can't go around killing people."

"He killed Jesús."

"I know, but *Tía*, the cops will get him."

"They don't ever get nobody! People just shoot and stab each other, and they don't care!" Tears slid down her face. She muttered her son's name over and over.

I looked down at the lawn. I pictured the police with their blue helmets and the kid on the tricycle muttering, "It ain't nice to say *bitch*."

My *tía* sank with a groan into the webbings of the lawn chair. Her eyes were moist. I touched her shoulder and wanted to rock her in my arms. Instead, I squeezed her shoulder. She pleaded with me and then turned to the two kids playing with plastic bats.

"Who are those kids?" she asked.

"Just some punks."

She sighed. She patted the dish towel full of tortillas. She asked me if I remembered how Jesús and I used to play in her yard, and how she used to fill us up with milk shakes.

"Yeah, I remember," I said flatly.

"You and Jesús."

"Yeah, yeah," I said. "We were so close." I was tired of my aunt and tired of trying to keep on a straight line.

33

"Then why don't you help me? Angel says he knows who did it."

Angel. I pictured him in Mr. Stiles's truck, one hand on the wheel and the other raising a joint to his face.

"Auntie, man, Angel is no good."

"He was Jesús's friend."

Yeah, right, I thought. I turned my head toward the noise of the two kids. I wanted to yell at them to shut up.

My *tía* unwrapped the red dish towel, exposing not a stack of tortillas but a handgun as large as a plumber's pipe wrench, maybe just as heavy.

"Jesus!" I cried. "What are you doing with that?"

She held it up for me to take. Her eyes were pink. She sobbed, "Take it, *mi'jo*. You and Angel can do it."

I turned my back to her and walked away, up the driveway until I was in the front yard. I walked to the end of the street and then started jogging. It was truly dusk. The east was one large bruise that was slowly becoming the night.

CHAPTER 3

The good life is one where you go to work, do an eight-hour shift, and return home to your family, where your kids are wild for you. After all, you're the daddy. Mountains rise from your shoulders, coins jingle in your pocket, and the food on the table is your doing. A good life is a long, busy evening of watching TV, where every third or fourth joke is actually funny. Maybe you throw down a beer, play checkers with your oldest kid, or kick back on the lawn when it's hot and all the dogs on the block have something to say to the moon. You don't care if the mosquitoes on your neck set their needle-thin heads into a vein. You want to share your blood, share because you're a young father and you got lots more where that came from.

What did I know? The working life was a scam. I could stencil every curb in Fresno from pagan Monday to holy Sunday, tattoo them with numbers so that no one, drunk or sober, could ever get lost. But no matter how hard I tried to live a straight life, I could still mess up.

I got out of bed, drank water like a horse, and pulled a box of Wheaties from the cupboard. I shook the box, which rattled like *maracas*, the sound of something half empty. I poured a bowl and splashed milk on those wimpy-ass flakes, remembering when I ate boatloads of Wheaties and believed they would make me a man one day. It didn't work.

I was rowing my spoon from the bowl to my mouth when a knock sounded on the front door. Mr. Stiles? The Wheaties clogged my throat, like a ball of wet cotton. I tiptoed to the window and parted the blinds. Angel was ready to strike the door again with his fist. And he did, hammering like a judge and rattling the window.

I opened the door and the heat of May was in my face, the heat and a jumpy Angel.

"Hey, Eddie, *mi carnal*!" Angel said cheerfully as he pushed himself into the living room. Once inside, he looked around nervously, his eyes like the eyes of a rabbit with a bullet in its throat.

"What's going on?" I asked. Last night, after my *tía* left, after she rewrapped the .22 pistol in the tortilla dish towel and walked crying to her car, I lay in bed thinking that Angel had stolen the truck. He could do things like that, steal from his friends, and then shrug his shoulders and look hurt when you accused him. But I accused him before he could say another word. "What did you do with the truck?"

"What?"

"The truck, man!" I was breathing on him, like the oven that was outside my front door. "You stole my truck!"

"Steal? Steal from an old school friend like you?" Angel smiled as he strolled to the kitchen. He looked inside the refrigerator for a soda. When he didn't find one, he closed it and wrung his hands under the kitchen faucet. He cupped them to drink, burped, and wiped his mouth on the front of his T-shirt. "I didn't steal no truck. I snagged an Acura."

A chill made the hairs on my arms stand at attention.

"And where'd you get a truck anyway?" Angel continued.

I didn't answer. For a brief moment I saw Mr. Stiles standing on his small, wind-whipped hill, the wilting flowers with their petals like ragged skirts. I asked, "Is it outside?"

"What?"

"Don't play around, homes. The Acura."

"Yeah, Eddie, the machine's parked outside," he said, waving vaguely.

"I don't want you here," I told Angel in a near whisper.

He sat down on the table and sneered at the cereal bowl, where two flies sat like sentries. Angel blew on the flies, but the flies gripped the bowl, not ready to give up the sweetness of a free meal.

"I got a plan, homes."

"Right," I said. "You got a plan to leave."

"You're a real comedian, Eddie boy." Angel laughed and pushed his hand into the box of Wheaties and brought out a handful of crushed flakes. "You and me can break down that Acura or sell the whole *pinche* thing to the Hmongs."

I sat down at the other end of the table. Angel wasn't stupid, just scary. He was good with figures and he'd been pretty smart until he got to fifth grade and started sniffing glue and spray paint.

"Check this out," he said. He brought out the

.22 pistol, the one my aunt had tried to shove on me.

"Angel!" I screamed as I stood up, the chair sliding back. "Get out of here!"

He stood up with the pistol in one hand. His other hand was stuffed in the Wheaties box. He grinned. "Your aunt came over last night and told me to blast the *vato*."

I pictured my aunt with mascara bleeding from her eyes.

"And she gave me some tortillas."

I pictured the tortillas wrapped in a dish towel.

"You got to go, Angel," I said, trying the be-nicer tactic.

"Can I have the Wheaties?" Angel asked with a grin. He shoved the pistol in the box, laughed the laugh of a homie on drugs, and tottered in the doorway for a moment before walking down the length of my driveway. I followed him, barefoot. I could see the heat as vapors rose from the black asphalt.

Angel turned to me and said, "Know what? You're a sissy." I could see him wavering, like the heat on the road, and I thought that maybe he was shooting up juice. I glanced down at his arms where spider bites would show like puckers. There were no signs.

"Yeah," I told Angel. "I'm a sissy. I'm everything you say."

Angel sneered. He carried the Wheaties cereal box like a briefcase as he made his way down the short driveway to his Acura.

At City College I sold my air-conditioning textbooks and got thirty-four dollars for them, a better price than

I'd expected, considering that the semester was nearly over. I bought a soda in the cafeteria. The cashier was a girl I went to school with, Norma.

"What's going on, homeboy?" she said, and stretched out her hand for my payment.

Not wanting to touch her, not interested in getting the least involved, I let the coins roll from my hands into her palm.

"Just kicking back," I said with a bob of my head. "Working."

She lifted her eyebrows, wanting to hear about my job. I didn't want to tell her that I was painting curbs for a living. Instead I told her I was painting houses.

"Heard about your *primo*," she remarked softly. Her eyes were blue with eyeshadow and her lipstick was pale. She looked like a vampire. She looked good. "You going to do something about it?"

I shrugged. I asked her how long she'd been working in the cafeteria. She said two weeks. She said if I wanted to snag a free sandwich, I could.

"Just help yourself, boy," she said with a smile, and I wasn't sure if she was talking about a sandwich or herself.

"Nah, I just want something to drink," I said. But I did look over at the sandwiches, caged in hard plastic and probably assembled by that guy named Bobby from my air-conditioning class. Dumb as a dog, he had gotten a good job pasting tuna and plunking down a coin-shaped pickle slice and a bloodless tomato on three kinds of bread. "I used to like him—your *primo*," she said. After a short hesitation she added, "He sort of looked like you."

"Jesús looked like me?"

Norma smiled and said, "Your eyelashes." She turned to face a new customer, a fat boy with a hamburger, the canned soup of the day, and a pile of crackers.

"Come by, Eddie," she told me without looking up. "You know where I live. I got a pool."

I took my soda outside and sat on the patio, where students mingled. I spied the mortuary students, all of them with cups of coffee and textbook manuals about stuffing the dead with liquids. I drained my soda, rolled the ice from the cup into my mouth, and spit it back. I opened the campus newspaper, a rag four pages long, and was reading a classified ad about giving pints of blood when I saw a Mexican guy at another table cross his legs—yellow shoes the color of a pat of butter. He was crowing with two chicks, crowing a good line because one of the girls was smiling and pumping her leg.

"Punk," I said under my breath. I let my mind go wild with violent options, for Mr. Yellow Shoes seemed like a dude who could ice someone, stick a knife into a chest and step back quickly to watch the blood flow red as a scarf. I waited for him to finish with the girls. When he got up, I got up, stretched, and followed him like a real Sherlock Holmes. He headed toward a classroom, and I followed him in when I saw that the class was large, like a hundred people, all of them giving off a vapor of sweat and onion. I trailed his butter-colored shoes and sat three rows behind him, next to a girl in a cowboy shirt.

"What kind of class is this?" I asked.

"What?"

"What kind of class is this?" I repeated, this time

louder, almost with anger. I wet my lips and said, "I'm thinking about taking it next year."

The girl told me that it was health ed. When the teacher walked in the door, I was surprised to see that he weighed about three hundred pounds. His middle-income lifestyle was showing around his waist. His hands were large enough to swat a brushfire.

I listened to the teacher for fifteen minutes, and as far as I could tell, he was talking about the rise and fall and rise again of TB. The guy hiked up his pants every two minutes, hiked them up and then swatted a hand at his sweaty face. I had to chuckle to myself. The guy didn't know what real work was, but there he was, sweating over saying some stupid words.

It was just like high school. Most of the students were not listening. Some were talking, others sleeping so soundly that you could drop a rock down their open mouths. A couple in the back was swapping tongues.

When class ended, I followed El Yellow Shoes. He returned to the cafeteria and drained a soda with another girl. He soon left, and for a moment I thought of scooting over to where Mr. Yellow Shoes had been sitting and crowing with the girl. Instead I followed him to his car, a Ford Escort, in the parking lot. He was a real schoolboy, dressed nicely, throwing off the good aroma of aftershave, and swinging his books back and forth. At any moment I thought he might start whistling. As he approached his car, I picked up my pace and called out, "You like to dance, homes?"

He looked around, not sure where the voice was coming from. There were students milling in the parking lot.

"You like to dance?" I said, not so politely. Even

if he didn't kill Jesús, I didn't like his yellow shoes and his white-boy outfit. I had my moments of gangster mentality, and this was one of them. I was fired up to get in his face.

"What?" There was first a dull look in his eyes and then a flash of terror.

"¿Y qué? Do I have to repeat myself?"

His eyes moved in his tear-slicked sockets.

"You packing?" I asked, now up into his face. If he had a knife or gun, I would have been dead right there in the parking lot, my blood another stain on the oily asphalt. He leaned away from me when I asked, "Did you do Jesús?"

I was so close to him that from a distance people might have thought we were friends. "I don't know no Jesús," he stuttered.

"Don't give me that!" I growled. "Everybody knows someone named Jesús."

"I don't know no Jesús."

"Like shit!"

He shook his head, which stank of cigarette smoke and mousse. I leaned closer to him and stepped on the tips of his shoes. I ground my shoes on top his, and if he had struggled, I would have broken his neck right there, one hand behind his back and the other coming swiftly up into his chin.

"Why did you kill Jesús?" I asked. Beneath his white-boy shirt, I could see a crucifix, our poor Savior with his head down and not feeling too good. They had lowered the boom on him centuries ago, and now everyone wanted a piece of the holy action. For Mr. Yellow Shoes, it was probably costume jewelry.

"I don't know no Jesús," he stuttered. He wanted to run, but with me stepping on his shoes and one arm resting on top of his shoulder, he had nowhere to go.

Over his shoulder, I spotted campus cops walking toward us. I repeated myself. "Why did you kill Jesús?"

He shook his head. Somewhere inside his head, the machinery that makes tears was kicking into action because his eyes were suddenly wet. I climbed off his shoes and turned, not in the least scared that he might jump me. I walked away, sweat cupped in my armpits and my breath wild with some force that could have broken the world in half.

A week later, I tugged out a piece of paper that had been slipped in the crack of the door at my apartment. The note was from Mr. Stiles, and he was asking for his truck back—no harm done, let's-be-friends kind of attitude. I crumpled the note in my hand and looked over my shoulder. A neighbor was starting up his lawn mower. Two kids across the street were jumping in the sprinklers. A dog was spurting his juice on a lowly bush.

"Man," I whispered to myself. I was stunned that he had found me, and found me so soon. I felt for the outline of the keys in my pants pocket. They were there, useless.

I opened the front door and stepped in slowly. Mr. Stiles could be inside, waiting. I figured that if he was there, I would let him wale on me as a sort of punishment, wale on me just for a few seconds before I started my action and hit back. Why was I to blame? The city was teeming with thugs, thieves, and low-IQ killers.

But there was no one there, just a few flies doing figure eights in the dank air. I turned on the swamp cooler and got a pitcher of ice water from the refrigerator. I chugged it standing up and let some of the water run down my chest, just like Rambo would do when he came in from doing battle in his own savage jungle.

The telephone started ringing. I looked at it, knowing that it was my aunt. I let the telephone howl and changed into a clean T-shirt, one with a paint stain near the heart. At the kitchen table, I wrote a note to Mr. Stiles: "Mr. Stiles, you won't believe it, but your truck got stole in front of my place and I didn't do it, sir. I think this guy I use to know in school did it, but I'm not sure about that. You got to trust me. I don't know what to say. I mean, I can't pay for your truck. Maybe you can find it. You saw me work at your house, and I mean this from my heart when I say that I'm sorry. Here are your keys back. Maybe the Hmongs did it."

I left the note unsigned. I folded the note in an envelope, dropped in the keys, and licked the edge, slamming it closed with a pound of my fist. When the telephone started again, I left the apartment and walked down Fruit Street to the bus stop, where a wino was seated, his hand around the throat of a tall cold one in a crumpled paper bag. His eyes were watery.

"Did you go to war?" he asked in a big-time slur.

I looked away, not in the mood for talking to winos.

The wino repeated himself, and I told him, "Calm down, man. Just drink your grog." He smacked his lips and took a birdlike swig. I couldn't help but think of what the mortuary students would do with a body like his—wrap it in all the paper bags he had drunk from and fire him up?

"I was in the war," he said.

I hugged my body in the rake-thin shadow of the bus shelter. All I wanted was to get on the bus, not to argue the pros and cons of war.

When the bus slowed, sighing to a stop, I hopped on and dropped in my coins—dimes, nickels, and pennies. The wino got on and sat in the back. I looked directly at him, but he didn't know who I was. His eyes were leaking memory right in front of me.

I rode up to the north section of Fresno, intending to leave my note at Mr. Stiles's house. I felt bad for him. He was a good guy, and I wanted him to know that I didn't mean him harm. I thought of ripping open the envelope and scrawling, "I'll help you find it." I fought the urge, even when the keys inside the envelope jingled like a bell.

I got off without thanking the bus driver or looking back at the wino. Heat wavered from the black asphalt.

"Damn," I said to myself. Sweat was kicking up on my brow.

From the bus stop, I had to walk nearly a mile. I felt like an ant under a toy magnifying glass—the heat was turning up the juice now that it was three o'clock. I cut across a field, knee-deep in tough weeds, stumbling over boards and dismantled bicycles. In a year or so a subdivision would go up there, with houses the color of crabmeat, off-white, or the color of crabs themselves, pink.

I started up the street where I had first searched for curbs to stencil. I took a right on the street where I helped the old dude with the air conditioner and was surprised to see a knot of people. There was an ambulance idling in the driveway and a monstrous fire engine. As I slowly approached the house, they were rolling a gurney down the driveway. The old man was lying there, with twin tubes in his nostrils. His wife followed him, crying behind her sunglasses, crying when only two weeks ago she had been jumping on him because she had promised the air conditioner to some woman named Barbara.

"What's happening?" I asked a teenage boy straddling a bike and sucking on a snow cone.

"I think he's dead."

The gawkers made room for the gurney and the wife, but still craned their necks for a look at old age on a white hospital sheet. Me, I looked in the garage. The air conditioner was still there.

"Hey, mister," a kid called to me.

The voice belonged to the kid with blue eyes, the one who'd thought I had said *bitch*. I didn't think twice. I walked away but the kid followed me on his squeaky tricycle.

"You stole the truck!" he yelled out. "My mom said you stole it!"

I didn't bother to look back to see if the gawkers

were paying attention. I hurried away, almost running. When I turned the corner toward Mr. Stiles's house, I glanced over my shoulder. The little blue-eyed creep wasn't following me. I felt for the envelope in my back pocket and scolded myself for being such a good Boy Scout. I should have just tossed the keys in the trash and forgotten about it.

"Man, it's ugly in this heat," I muttered to myself. I backhanded sweat from my eyes and leaned my face into a sprinkler that was going full blast on a newly planted sod lawn.

Mr. Stiles's front yard was as barren as a pitcher's mound. The birch tree we had planted was no more than a blind-man's cane jabbed in the ground. The flowers in the beds had folded in on themselves. The place looked dry and all hope seemed to have disappeared.

I'm sorry, Mr. Stiles, I thought, and hurried across the half-finished landscape, placing the envelope on the welcome mat. I knew no one was home—the air-conditioning was off and the garage door was closed. I thought of peeking in the window, just to see what kind of home he was putting together, but I didn't. I turned on my heels and almost skipped from the shadowy porch.

I heard a child's voice cry out, "Mister, you're a bitch."

The tyke on the trike was coming up the sidewalk, his pinkish knees churning. He was a regular cop. If he'd had a handgun at his waist, he would have clipped me right there.

I hustled away and could see two curtains part,

then a third, while the kid continued after me, mouth open to baby teeth and crying out, "You plant bitch stuff."

At my apartment I leaned against the refrigerator. I had had to race my ass out of that subdivision and hide in the weeds when the cops were called to look for a thief, meaning me. I'd hid in the weeds and felt like crying because I was spread out, facedown, on a pile of grass clippings and what I imagined were buried onions.

I chugged ice water and then put it away when I heard a knock on the front door.

"Angel, you lowlife," I said to myself. I made a halfhearted decision not to answer it, but when I sneaked a peek through the window, I knew for sure that I wasn't going to open the door: It was my mom with my aunt Gloria, in Fresno for god knows what reason. They were leaning their ears to the door, like spies. I stayed cool, but when the door jingled with a key, I remembered that my mom had an extra key.

"Mi'jo," my mom called. "It's us."

The two women entered the apartment, and I adopted a surprised look. "Oh, I was in the bathroom," I said.

The two of them inspected the apartment, which was bare as a gnawed bone. My mom was in her fifties, an old mom considering that she was Mexican and most Mexican mothers I knew had their first kids when they were sixteen. After my father died, she went from a young woman to a middle-aged woman to an old woman in a matter of months it seemed. She even retired early from PG & E and started hogging all the senior discounts—theater tickets, bus passes, restaurant food. And she looked old, in a print dress and black shoes, with a bud of wrinkles around her whiskery mouth. She played up the *abuelita* image, except that she had no grandkids.

"You got some coffee, *mi'jo*?" Mom asked. She was already stepping toward the kitchen. "It's *cochino*, so dirty here."

"Nah, Mom," I said, and then smarted off, "I think the cockroaches had Bible study here last night."

My aunt Gloria held her tongue. She didn't want to lash me with criticism, at least not yet. She had to have a cup of coffee in her hand before she would pick me apart.

The two women searched my cupboards for a coffee can, and when they didn't find one, they sat down at the kitchen table, sweeping away crumbs and two wandering ants. I didn't have much to offer, just ice water. I was even out of Kool-Aid.

"Here," my mom said.

From her purse, she brought out a huge, foil-wrapped burrito. It seemed at least two times as large as her purse.

I unwrapped it, but I knew it was impolite to eat in front of people without grub in their own hands. When my mom said that they had had dinner, I dug into the burrito. This boy was hungry.

Then my aunt started in. "How come you got no girlfriend?"

"They're all married," I answered.

"No, that's not true," my aunt countered. "Do you know Norma?"

"I know a ton of Normas. They're all over the place."

"Norma Rodriguez. You know her?"

I shook my head. I was halfway done with my burrito.

"Norma is a really pretty girl, and she's only got one baby."

"She ain't married?"

"No, she had a baby in high school, and I don't know what happened to the boy."

I was down to a quarter burrito.

"Yeah, *mi'jo*," my mom started in. "I saw her, and she's really pretty. The baby looks like her."

"That's good, Mom." The burrito was now a pinch of tortilla in my hands.

"You should find a girl," my aunt Gloria repeated.

"*Tía*, it's hard enough just to live on my own." I pointed toward the kitchen. "You saw my cupboards."

The women fell silent and beady-eyed as two crows on a wire. They looked at each other and then my mom started in again. "*Míra*, I have a picture of Norma."

"Mom, I ain't interested."

"She's pretty," my mom argued as she fumbled in her purse. She shoved the Kmart photo into my face and I, trying to be a nice son, raised my eyebrows in interest. She looked OK, but her smile was like a sneaky sneer.

My mom rummaged through her purse. She brought out a stack of vanilla wafers and offered them first to Aunt Gloria, who declined with a wave of her hand, and then to me. I took one, rolled out my tongue, and placed it there like it was a host.

50

"Don't be like that," my mom scolded. "God is going to punish you."

"I thought he was already doing that."

"You don't know what hell is."

My aunt Gloria wagged her head. "It's true. Me and your mommy know what hell is. And Jesús's mom, *su tía* Dolores. *Pobrecita.* All you boys are going to kill each other!"

"How come?" Mom snapped. "How come you're killing each other? You think it's funny." Mom spit a crumb of vanilla wafer in my direction.

"I didn't do anything," I argued. "Why jump on my case?"

"It's so sad for Dolores," my mom said, pretty sad herself. Absentmindedly she slipped a vanilla wafer into her mouth. "I know that she wants you to hurt that boy, but I want you to stay away, *mi'jo.*"

My aunt Gloria took a wafer, too, and told us how she remembered Jesús when he was a boy and *un travieso.* She told us that he had once taken the cigarette lighter in the car and burned holes on the plastic dashboard.

We sat in silence, water dripping in the sink, and then my mom said, "*Míra.*" She turned the side of her face to me; there was a wormlike hearing aid lodged in her ear. "I got this a month ago. Just like Gloria's."

Aunt Gloria nodded. "From Sears."

"I thought your hearing was OK."

"It's no good, *mi'jo.* I can't hear no more."

My mom took it out from her ear and put it in her outstretched palm. The hearing aid looked like a snail. Then she said, "Try it on!"

"¡*Chale*!" I jumped out of my chair as she shoved

51

the thing in my face. These women were *viejas locas.*
They laughed, but stopped laughing when the telephone began to ring. I looked at it but didn't pick it up. All I needed was Aunt Dolores to hear my mom in the background and come over with a pot of coffee. The women would gab until morning.

"Get it!" Mom commanded as she shoved the hearing aid back into her ear, ready for *chisme.*

When I stood up and made for the kitchen to get a glass of water, my mom sighed, struggled to her feet, and scooted toward the phone snoring its sixth ring.

"Let it ring, Mom," I shouted. "It ain't nobody."

She picked it up, either because her hearing aid was off or I was her son and in no position to boss her around.

"Hello," she said in her Spanish-heavy accent. She looked confused, just like a *vato* coming down from sniffing glue. "Norma?"

"Is it Norma . . . Rodriguez?" Aunt Gloria asked with eyes peeled open. She was swallowing a second vanilla wafer.

"No, it's another Norma," Mom answered, and then shoved the telephone at me. "It's for you!"

"I thought you didn't have no girlfriend," Aunt Gloria remarked. She took the hearing aid from her ear and turned up the volume.

I took the telephone and crowed into the receiver, "Yeah?" I eyed my mom and aunt, their eyes bright and heads nodding, so happy that a girl was calling me.

But they didn't know who was on the other end of the line. It was Norma from high school, Norma the cafeteria cashier, Norma with the tattoo tear. It was

Norma who at quarter to nine on a night of two nagging women wanted me to come over and enjoy a swim in her pool.

I said a couple of *yeah*s to Norma. I took down her address, hung up, and said, "Mom, a friend needs my help." I hurried to my bedroom and pulled out my bathing suit and walked past the women, who followed me outside yelling, "Is she pretty?"

I yelled back, "Lock up!" and disappeared into the night of gunfire and howling dogs.

CHAPTER 4

Norma offered me a soda and two sandwiches she'd snatched from work. I ate them by her pool, which shimmered under an orange porch light. She offered me her neck, too, and I gladly accepted it, putting down my own dark love *placa*. She moaned. She said that I reminded her of Jesús, my dead cousin, and I didn't care that she made the comparison. I had food to eat and a place to throw my *besos*. She was misted over with perfume, but I could taste the salt on her neck and shoulders. I struggled to bring down a strap from her swimsuit, but she fought me off playfully, saying that I was a naughty boy. So I fed my hunger on her neck and her shoulder. We traded tongues and then I was back to her neck. I didn't pull my face away until she said through a moan, "You know that Angel did it, don't you?"

I pushed her away and looked at her. "What do you mean?"

She didn't answer. "You're just like Jesús," she whispered. Her tongue was a flickering flame on my ear.

I made her stop and repeated, "What do you mean about Angel and Jesús?"

Norma quickly cooled. In the glare of the porch

light, with her tattoo tear, she looked like a vampire. Her eyeteeth shone. Her hair was mussed.

"Jesús was so nice," Norma said.

"Don't kid yourself," I said. "Jesús was a gangster like everybody else."

"But he was nice."

I didn't say anything to this. We sat at the pool's edge, our feet in the water. She kicked her legs girlishly and the light on the surface broke like glass.

"I don't believe you," I told her after a moment of silence. Evil as he was, I couldn't see Angel doing Jesús like that. Maybe someone else, but not Jesús.

"It's all around. Everyone knows, Eddie." She told me that she had heard the rumor—the *chisme*—from homies at Holmes playground. She said that Jesús was mad because they had stolen a car together and Angel sold it but didn't split the profits.

"You ain't making this up?" I asked.

She shook her head. Her eyes were large, stamped with so much of the ugly world.

I jumped to my feet. My heart pounded at the thought that Angel had plunged a knife into Jesús, his *carnal*, or at least the friend he kicked around with. Now he had a gun, my aunt's, and I thought that he would use it as easily as he would brush his teeth.

"Don't tell anyone I told you," Norma said. Her eyes were even bigger.

I lowered myself into the pool and then pushed myself back up on the edge, water falling off in sheets. I had to cool off.

"You won't, will you?" Norma pleaded.

"Nah, girl." I figured that I would play dumb, my usual role, and not let on that I knew.

Norma kicked her leg in the water, and even though she looked good sitting at the edge of the pool, her breasts like pillows, I knew I had to get out of there.

"See ya," I said to Norma. I grabbed my clothes and jumped a small chain-link fence. I figured that I might have to get used to jumping fences.

The streetlight threw out a medicine-colored glare on the asphalt street. Like a cat, I kept to the shadows and didn't speak up when I saw three Hmongs easing a wire hook inside a car window. Break-ins were as common as yawns. Nothing new in Fresno.

My apartment was quiet as a shoe and just as smelly. All the windows were locked up. I flung two open and then turned on the swamp cooler, but kept the lights out. The moonlight flooded the dining table, where I spotted about three dollars in coins. Under the coins there was a scrawled note from my mom that read, "*Mi'jo*, you go get some coffee tomorrow."

In bed I slept some, but I mostly lay listening for sounds of footsteps. When I woke just after seven, my eyes felt raw. I got up, the mattress groaning under the weight of my body. Since there was no coffee, I drank water. I rattled a box of raisins in the cupboard, opened the flap, and tossed them into my mouth.

"The dream life," I joked to myself.

I sat on my couch, a hand-me-down from my mom, and would have sat there all day, except a knock on the front door spooked me. I jumped to my feet and crept across the floor. I pecked out the blinds and saw somebody in uniform. At first I thought, The police, but when I saw the stripe on his sleeve, I realized that it was the military. I thought, Shit, man, they're here to recruit me. I was suddenly filled with hope.

When I pulled open the door, the smiling soldier yelled, "Border patrol, homes," grabbed me by the throat, and pushed me hard to the wall. My eyes almost leapt from my sockets and my tongue flapped like a lizard's tail. He held me there until he had his fill of tough-guy tactics. Chuckling, he let me go.

It was José Dominguez, a friend from school I used to sniff glue with. He was a cop in the marines and had learned a lot of in-close fighting techniques that could mess up people for life. After my eyes cleared and my tongue fixed itself back into place, I punched him for real in the stomach. José took it with a stutter step backward, and with a grin bellowed, "You can't hurt this soldier, homes."

It was too early in the morning to bother with him. I went back to the couch, swallowing and feeling the damage to my throat.

"What are you doing here?" I croaked. I picked up a newspaper and rolled it up. A black fly circled the air.

"I'm on leave."

"You're on leave, and you come back to this hole?" I swallowed and then said, "You messed up my throat."

"I didn't even touch you. If I had touched you, you woulda known." José glanced around my apartment. "How come you're living in this cave?"

I ignored him. I busied myself with the fly. I whacked at the air and missed. I told José, without much conviction, "I'm doing OK."

"You look like shit, homes," he told me. "When's the last time you ate?"

I didn't say that breakfast was water and raisins. I took another swipe at the fly and missed.

"Come on," José whined. "Let's go out for breakfast—Cuca's or Mama Luisa's?"

I got up, ran a razor over the baby stubble on my face, and slipped into a T-shirt with a Champion spark plug on the front.

José and I had kicked around since junior high when we pulled together our first peewee gang, the Impalas. We scratched our *placas* in wet cement, tagged walls and signs, and occasionally ripped off bikes from crybaby kids. We would have stayed friends, except he moved across town. We didn't meet up again until we were at Roosevelt High, and by then he was a wrestler and had changed. He was clean-cut, just like now. He liked uniforms back then, and apparently he still liked them. You'd never have guessed that we had tripped around Fresno sniffing glue from paper bags. Now he was a marine with cropped hair.

"You got a ride?" I asked as we stepped into the sunlight. I peeked around cautiously as we strolled up the driveway toward the street. No telling where Angel could be hiding with his cannon.

"I got my dad's car," José said as his hands swung at his sides as if he were marching. "He had a heart attack."

"Ah, that's too bad," I said, meaning it. Mr. Dominguez had been a *suave* guy. One time he'd taken us to the lake, where he got drunk and passed out. We snagged the empty cans and downed the leftover piss-colored beer.

"He's OK," José said. "He just can't work no more. Or drink."

For one greedy second I thought of asking José where his dad worked. Maybe I could get his job if it was still open. But I just swallowed and rubbed my throat, which still hurt from his grip.

We hopped into his father's cheap Dodge Colt and took off with the speed and noise of a lawn mower. Blue smoke hung in the air.

On the way over to Cuca's, José told me about the marines—from the day they buzzed his hair to the hand-to-hand combat with real bayonets. He told me that he had gained fifteen pounds and put on a boat-load of muscles. He said even his butt muscles got hard.

"No way!" I laughed.

"Feel it, if you don't believe it," he told me.

"In your dreams, homes."

He told me then, seriously, that he was being shipped out, destination unknown because it was top secret. He wanted to kick around Fresno one more time.

I clicked my tongue at this top-secret stuff. He was playing games.

"You know, homes," José said as we moved over the bumpy tracks to the west side. "You know, I won't be eating any Mexican food for a long time."

I didn't say anything. My stomach was already caved in. The topic of food only made it worse.

We drove in silence, the Dodge Colt doing alright once it got going. Then José asked, "You ain't doing too good, huh?"

"I could be doing worse."

I told him about my poor cousin now on his rack of black earth, and José just shook his head, whistled, and said, "I guess you could be messing up worse."

He asked me who had done Jesús, and I just shrugged my shoulders and said, "Someone."

At a red light, some punk kids saluted José with a *pinche* finger, and José returned it with a grin. He pulled the Colt away with its lawn-mower growl.

"Yeah, once you're dead, you're dead," I said of my poor cousin.

"*De veras.* I saw some films in boot camp. Stuff the public never sees."

"Yeah? Like what?"

"You know, films about safety, so we don't go around doing dumb shit." He described how they were herded into an auditorium and shown clips of injured and dead marines, all maimed by their own stupid errors—or so the sergeant barked.

José talked about a guy who sliced off his chin with a bayonet and another who, for a joke, stuffed a bullet in his nostril, tripped, and blew out his left eye. I half listened with my eyes peeled for Angel.

"Yeah, bro. It's tough in the marines!"

"You get to eat good, no?"

"Chocolate milk seven days a week," he crowed. "They got a brown cow back there in the kitchen."

Then José started in about how he had to club drunk marines. He said he was bad. I was already tired of his macho shit about marines, but I stayed quiet. It was a free breakfast, and I knew that José, deep down in his heart, was OK.

Before we got to the restaurant, José drove by Leticia's house. Leti was José's girl for three years, but they broke up when she caught him with Norma. He honked the horn and when he saw the curtain part, he waved, laughed, and drove away.

"You didn't get over her, huh," I said.

"You mean, she didn't get over me."

I could see that José was still bothered about Leti. But it was his love life, not mine.

At Cuca's we got first-rate service, not only because we knew the owners but also because José was wearing his uniform. He stood tall and clean, not like me, a rag dipped into a pail of soapy water.

"It's tough being a marine," he told the owner, a woman my mom and every Mexican in Fresno knew.

"You look so handsome." *La señora* smiled.

José beamed.

We ordered the works, *chile verde* with a couple of eggs on top. Plus sodas. As we finished our grub, a shirtless black dude with red eyes came into the restaurant. I sized up his arms for needle tracks, but his veins weren't tattered with pucker marks. I assumed he was homeless.

"People, I got onions!" he shouted. "You need 'em, ma'am?"

He directed his attention to the owner, who waved him off as she muttered in Spanish. The black dude turned next to a *Tejano* returning from the rest room to his seat.

"Nah, we ain't interested in onions," *la señora* Cuca repeated as she rubbed down the counter. Her patience was up. "You gotta go!"

"They're real good," the dude said.

"No! Go! *¡Ándale!*" *La señora* waved a dish towel at him.

The dude looked around the small restaurant, where the patrons were eating slowly and waiting for him to leave. They didn't spend good money to watch the homeless hustle onions.

"Onions," he repeated, this time quieter. "Whole sack of onions for three dollars."

When José called him over with a nod of his head, the dude hustled over and said, "Twenty-pound sack for three dollars. A good deal!"

I could smell his sweat and the iron scent of someone desperately waiting for a sale.

"Where did you get the onions, man?" José asked.

"I found 'em."

José and I knew that he snagged them from the fields.

"I found 'em on the road," he added, pointing vaguely at the door. He looked from me to José and then said, "You a marine?"

"What do you think?"

"You kill anybody?"

"No, man. I ain't into hurting people."

The black dude looked at the smeared faces of our plates. "I need money, man. I got onions, and my family is hungry."

José rolled an ice cube into his mouth and said, "I'll be outside in a sec."

"Be quick, sir," the black dude said as he walked backward. "It's hot as hell out there."

He left the restaurant calling out one last time, "Onions!"

Stuffed, José and I sat in our booth and watched a fly walk back and forth, like a sentry. I told José that the fly was him, a marine fly.

"*¡Chale!* In the marines we got flies three times as large. That fly looks like it belongs in the air force."

José paid. We left the restaurant and the sunlight was like a knife in our eyes. Bums, day laborers, and wanna-be gangsters hugged the dusty shadows of boarded-up businesses.

"It's hot," José said.

"Wait until three," I said. I turned when I heard the dude with the onions hiss, "Over here, my friend."

José fit his cap snugly on his head and walked toward the dude, who hustled us to the parking lot. He headed toward a car holding five children, two in the front and three in the back. The car, a huge Buick Electra, was a standard RV of poverty. The windows were greasy. The upholstery was throwing up its guts. One of the children, still in diapers, was howling.

"These be really good onions," the dude said. He opened the trunk of the car with a poke of a screwdriver into the hole where a lock had been. He lifted one bag and the car squeaked.

"Three dollars for a sack. Why don't you take five."

"What am going to do with five sacks?"

The man looked at José and said, "That's right, you a marine and going overseas. Am I right?"

José didn't want to rap with the guy. "Just give me two."

"Why not three?" He looked at me and remarked, "Your amigo could use some onions."

"I don't need a sack."

"It's vitamin C. Good stuff. Tasty with taters. How your kind of people call potatoes?"

"*Papas,*" José said. He seemed to be smiling, but

the smile was forced by the sun's glare. José wanted the deal over.

"Them! I ain't got 'em now but I can find 'em."

"Right in the road, huh?" José said.

José ended up buying three sacks of onions and then, a real soldier, handed a pack of Juicy Fruit to the kids in the car. The black dude thanked us a hundred times, even bowed, and with a sack in each hand, José led the way to the car. I carried the third sack, which felt heavy as a body.

We loaded the sacks in the trunk of the Dodge Colt and were getting ready to leave when I spotted Mr. Stiles's red Toyota across the street in front of the Azteca movie theater. Heat was wavering off its roof and hood.

"José!" I called. He nearly jumped out of his shoes.

"You think you calling Mexico? I'm standing right here. No reason to shout." José was bent down, checking out the front wheel. He stood up, spanking dust from his palms. "What?"

I told him about how I had worked for Mr. Stiles and had my truck—Mr. Stiles's truck—stolen right out from under me.

José scanned the block, his cap off.

"Let's go get it," José said after a moment.

"I don't know, man."

"Whatta you, scared?"

"Ain't you?"

José scanned the block again, this time more carefully. His gaze fell on two winos and the winos' dog. He opened up his car door and from underneath the seat brought out a crescent wrench. He threw me a screwdriver, which I turned over in my hands and examined.

"You know this dude Stiles's number?" he asked without looking at me. He had turned his attention to the truck.

I told him I did, and José said, "Call and tell him that you found his ride. Tell him to get down here and we'll wait for him."

In a flash I went back into Cuca's restaurant and used the pay telephone. Nervous, with sweat running like the Mississippi River down my brown face, I got Mr. Stiles on the third ring. He seemed groggy. When I started to explain where his truck was, he said with a cry in his voice, "I trusted you, Eddie."

"Mr. Stiles, I didn't mess you over," I said with a cry in my own voice. "It's the honest truth. I'll be waiting with the truck and I'll tell you how it was."

"Why did you do it, Eddie?" he cried. He was wide awake.

"I'm telling you, I didn't do it!" I told him I had gone to the dump, done my job, picked up a refrigerator, and when I took it home, someone snagged his truck. There was silence on his end. I pictured his house with its one tree on the front lawn. Birch tree/ bitch tree, I thought. I pictured his house and then the kid on the tricycle. Right there, at Cuca's, I had the feeling that cops were going to be involved. I saw myself down on the ground, legs splayed, a cop's boot three inches from my face.

I shook the image. I gave him the directions and told him if he wanted his truck to get down here. I hung up, my legs weak. I left the restaurant without eyeing anyone, not even *la señora*, who followed me with her gaze.

The sun was harsh and for a moment I couldn't see. I shaded my eyes and when I looked across the street to the red Toyota, I saw José bending over like he was checking a tire, except there was no tire. He was bending over and three guys—brown boys in green Dickies—were running. One turned and threw a bottle at José. The bottle missed but kicked up shattered glass.

"I'm going to get you!" I yelled, and ran across the street, searching for something to pick up. I was going to mess up those boys.

José was stabbed. He was down on one knee, blood in the shape of the United States on the sidewalk. The winos and their dogs came over to see if they could help.

"José!" I screamed over him, and undid his jacket. "I'll get 'em. I'll mess 'em away."

I laid him down on the sidewalk and he kicked his legs, like he was riding a bike. The blood seeped from his shoulder and near his waist. His eyes had collected tears and they were ready to race down his face. I don't know if they were tears of pain or tears of embarrassment from getting knifed by thirteen-year-old *changos*.

José bicycled his legs and rolled to his side. He tried to get up, but I held him down gently and told the winos to go to Cuca's for help and to get some towels and ice. They staggered away. The wino dogs followed, tails shaking.

"You shoulda waited," I cried.

In the distance, I heard the jingle of a *mexicano's* *paleta* cart and farther off, less sweet, the blowing siren of a cop car.

The next morning I left for the hospital, my head up not because I was feeling good but because I was keeping alert. No telling when someone was going to jam a knife in me. No telling when Angel would pull a gun from a paper bag and fire on me just as I crossed the street or bent down to tie my shoes.

"Nothin's right," I muttered to myself as the hospital door sighed open and the cool air replaced the warm, humid air. I noticed there were more people going in than coming out. It was a spooky thought. You show up at the hospital and don't get to leave.

I raced to the sixth floor. José was lying up there with tiny plastic hoses in his nose and IVs in his arms. Stitched up, drugged up, and slobbering on a clean pillow, José was going to make it.

José's family was there. I could feel that they thought it was my fault. I tried to tell them I had gone to make a telephone call and when I returned José had been stabbed. They looked away when I told them about the red Toyota truck and how José was going to help me. They knew it was my fault, and José was too groggy to stand by me. Carloads of relatives showed up. Even José's ex, Leti, showed up spilling tears. She cried into her hands, both tattooed, I saw, with José's initials. José's mother held her and Leti hugged her back. It was a regular feel-good session.

I walked back to Cuca's. Mr. Stiles's truck was

gone. I figured that he had come and gotten it, and he may or may not have looked down and seen José's dried blood. No telling.

I bought a Popsicle and examined my situation. I had returned the truck but at the cost of seeing my friend get knifed. I had traded headaches. Then there was Angel lurking somewhere in Fresno. At that moment he could have been beating someone with a pipe or pulling a holdup at a 7-Eleven.

With my Popsicle melting, I hurried to the bus stop. I kept my distance from the winos and the wino dogs. Ten minutes later I boarded a bus and got spooked again when I noticed there were more people getting on than getting off. We were all poor, all going somewhere. But where?

CHAPTER 5

I wanted to sprint straight into the future, but I kept going in circles. With a dirty face and hands curled into fists, I went back to Holmes playground. I encountered Lupe's little brother, Samuel, who was sitting on a bench with junior high *mocosos*, a chrome-colored boom box at their feet, along with a couple of crushed paper bags. They had been inhaling. When they saw me, they giggled and slurred their words when they asked me to buy them a soda.

"You seen Angel?" I growled. I was hot and angry. The long walk from the west side had dragged on the hard bones in my shoulders.

The young *cholos* nearly fell off the bench laughing idiotically. They were tripping on airplane glue. They giggled, and Samuel pointed toward the sky. Wrong, I thought. If Angel is going anywhere, it's down below. He's going to room with the devil, the *cholo* of all *cholos*.

I waved them off and went to the rec room, where Coach was propped up on a stool like a king. He was pumping up a basketball. I asked if he had seen Angel, but, ignoring me, he asked, "How's school?"

"I'm out already. It's stupid."

Coach was a good guy, a Vietnam vet, an ex-gang

banger with a swirl of tattoos running up both arms. He had been tough in his day but now, as rec leader, his job was pumping up basketballs and checking out checkers, chess, and a game called Sorry for the little kids. Now and then he got to stop fights, sometimes even getting a few blows in before the cops arrived for some fun of their own. He knew enough not to get on my case about dropping out of college.

"Help me, Eddie," Coach asked. "Do the lines."

"Where, Coach?"

He eased the needle from the basketball and pointed to the baseball diamond outside.

On Tuesday nights the playground was given over to league softball, usually your thirty-and-over white boys—carpenters, roofers, and tile layers, a bunch of born-again jocks with guts like sacks of cement. *Cholitos* used to break into their cars and sometimes even drive off in them, radios blaring. But it was harder these days. Now the playground hired security, those former bullies from high school who would rather see you dead on the ground than shake hands with you.

"Let me get you a soda," Coach said. He popped open the soda machine. I snagged some brown medicine, a Dr. Pepper, and gulped it down. I crushed the can, burping.

"I heard about José," Coach said, shaking his head and clicking his tongue in disgust. "You were there?"

"Yeah," I said in a low voice. An image of José on all fours and blood pouring from him like sand rolled across the back of my brain. "They hardly put him in the paper or anything. Just the regular bullshit."

On the obituary page, the *Fresno Bee* had written up a story about the stabbing, giving him—us—three inches, as deep as the knife had penetrated into José's body. They had mentioned my name as a witness, something I thought was stupid because the homies might come after me.

"That's sorry," Coach said.

I shrugged. What else was new?

While Coach continued pumping up basketballs, I got out the chalk machine, which is like a lawn mower but pours out an even two-inch-wide line of chalk to mark the area of play. When I was a punk third grader, an old gangster from the old days, the '60s, told me that they were lines of cocaine, and it scared me, a drug laid out like that and all of us gangsters ready to sniff it up like anteaters. Then he laughed and said it was just smashed chalk from all the teachers who had given up. That made me feel better.

I was doing the lines when Samuel and his friends staggered onto the diamond. They started kicking the lines, messing them up.

"You little punks," I yelled, furious.

They cussed at me and laughed the laughter of glue sniffers. They were still high, but I could see that they were coming down. I tried to scatter them by pushing the chalk machine at them, just short of clipping them at the knees. One stumbled, and the others jumped back, laughing. Then Samuel brought out a knife, the blade flashing like a car mirror.

"Eat this," he taunted. Ten feet away, he jabbed it at me. "You think you're too good for us."

Before I could kick his ass, Coach showed his face from the rec room, waving for Samuel and his homies to get away.

"Get outta here!" he shouted as he stomped onto the diamond. "You're suspended for two weeks!"

The homies cussed at Coach and ran across the lawn toward the parking lot. They stopped and gave us the finger. They were like vapors on the black asphalt.

"Little punks," Coach said. "I don't know if they're going to stay alive the way they act."

I left the playground with my job unfinished, and since I was only a few blocks away from my *nina*'s house, I decided to see her. I wanted to call my mom from there, to ask her to send me a money order so I could take the bus and visit her for a few weeks. I needed to distance myself from Fresno.

I crossed First Street, which was stained with the furry remains of two squirrels—*cholitos* of the animal kingdom. I jumped over their little bodies and then doused my sweaty face in a sprinkler set on a brown lawn. It was about three o'clock. The sun was pulling sweat from everything that moved—people, animals, and maybe insects, too.

"Shit, man," I growled to myself as I spotted Samuel and his homies at the end of the block. They were waiting for me, now with two knives blinking a chrome-colored light. They shouted something inaudible, probably stupid, and I turned away. While I wasn't scared of them, I didn't want to dirty myself with a round of *chingasos*. I skipped into an alley, where I raced through the glitter of broken glass and the debris of overturned garbage cans. I glanced back. They were after me. What a joke, I thought. I could crush all of them, but the thought of bloodying my

Aaron Li

knuckles on their ugly faces made me keep running.

"Low-class *cholos*," I muttered to myself.

I climbed a fence and dropped into a yard where an old woman was smoothing out wet laundry on a clothesline. The woman didn't hear me at first, but her eyes grew large in her wrinkled face when she saw me hunched against the fence, panting like a rabbit. She studied me for a moment and then listened to Samuel and his homies talking in the alley.

"*Señora*, they're after me," I whispered. I pursed my lips and lifted a finger to give her a hush sign.

But she dropped the wet laundry into her plastic basket and yelled, "Rubén! Rubén!" her wide-eyed stare locked on me. She was actively memorizing my face.

No mercy for me, I thought.

Her old man staggered into the gray shadow of the screen door on the back porch. He was shirtless, the bowl of his belly hanging over his belt. His hair was mussed, as if he had been drowsing. He shouted, "*¿Qué, Vieja?*"

The woman pointed in my direction.

He disappeared into the house, and I knew that he was either getting his gun or calling the police. I scrambled to my feet. When I made for the neighbor's yard, the woman bent down, picked up the wet laundry, and smacked me across the back. I pushed her away, almost knocking her down, and hopped over into the next yard, which started a pair of dogs, two crooked-teeth Chihuahuas, barking. Both of them were wearing filthy sweaters. The dogs barked, and I glanced at the back porch of the house. Sure enough, a woman's face appeared.

73

Like Flash Gordon, I jumped another fence and raced up a driveway onto a dead-looking street. The lawns were yellowish and the rose beds choked with weeds. There were kids in the shade of a porch playing cards. I walked quickly past them and they followed me with their eyes. One called me a nasty name, but at nineteen and with trouble mounting, I ignored the taunt. My life was worth more.

At the corner I hid against a huge sycamore tree, counting time and scraping bark from the trunk. I didn't see Samuel and his homies, or the shirtless old man. I could have crossed the street and leapt over those dead squirrels and back to the playground, where it was somewhat safe. I could have returned to my apartment and waited out Angel. At least I would know my enemy.

But my *nina*'s house was only three blocks away. I started toward there, swiftly but not running. I stripped off my T-shirt and tied it around my brow like a bandanna.

My *nina* appeared at the front window when I knocked. She peered first through the curtain, and after a few seconds of sizing me up, she opened the door, carefully. There were tears in her eyes, like the wetness on a leaf after a rain.

"What's wrong with your head?" she asked.

I untied the T-shirt and ignored her question. I asked her if I could use the telephone.

"Of course," she said, and opened the screen door.

Inside, I was grateful for the moist chill of the swamp cooler. The living room was dark with the curtains drawn against the heat, and the TV, volume turned down, gave off an eerie light that made the furniture glow. I glanced for a second at the program, a romantic *telenovela:* A daughter seemed upset with her mother whose face dripped tears.

"How come you're crying?" I asked.

"I'm taking Queenie to the pound," she answered slowly, as if she were reading the recipe on the back of a cereal box. A new flush of tears ran down her cheek. Queenie was so old, she said, that it would be better if she was put to sleep.

A chill ran down my arms, cooling off my anger at Samuel. I remembered Queenie, a mixed collie, when they first got her ten—no, way longer—years ago. She was a good dog, one who could snatch a Frisbee from the air. She could shake hands even. Her nuzzling nose was like love itself.

"I'm sorry," I said. I looked around the living room. "Where's is she?"

She said the dog was in the backyard. She asked me if I wanted a soda and I told her that would be nice.

While she went off to the kitchen, I used the telephone in the hallway, where the duct of the swamp cooler blasted air that was almost freezing. I called Merced, a town only fifty miles north of Fresno, punching in the numbers. I got my mom on the fifth ring, and when I said, almost yelling, "It's me, Mom," she asked, "Who?"

"Your no-good son," I screamed into the telephone. I remembered that she was sporting a hearing aid. So I added, "It's Eddie."

"Oh," she responded. "Are you at a car wash?"

The noise of the swamp cooler was loud.

"Nah, I'm at my *nina*'s," I screamed.

Then, instead of listening to me, or asking about José Dominguez, whom she must have read about in the newspaper, she asked if I had used the money she had given me to buy coffee. She was going to be in town in a week and wanted to be sure that I had coffee in my cupboard the next time she visited. She told me that she was so embarrassed that I didn't have anything to offer Aunt Gloria.

"Forget the coffee! I need you to send me twenty bucks. I gotta get out of this place!"

"But you gotta good job doing the curbs like you do," she said. "You say it's really good money."

"Mom, this is serious," I yelled. "I need money now! I want to stay with you for a couple of weeks."

She promised that she would go down to the post office after she had her hair done, meaning dyed and curled into some kind of old-lady look. Then I listened to her crow about how she had won ninety dollars in Reno, plus a Walkman stereo, which I could have if I painted the numbers on her and her *comadre*'s curb. The Walkman didn't have batteries, but she would buy me some if I washed all the screens on her windows. She had a two-for-one coupon good until the end of the month. When I couldn't stand it any longer, I told her that I was calling long-distance, sort of, and hung up after three or four good-byes and one "I love you, too, Mom."

My *nina* wasn't in the kitchen. I considered throwing open the refrigerator and snagging a handful of lunch meat, but I checked myself. I had to show some respect.

On the table sat my soda, a sugary medicine that I could take like a good soldier. I snapped it open and took it to the backyard. My *nina* was petting Queenie, who was shivering on a pink baby blanket. Her eyes were milkish white with cataracts, and a big patch of fur was gone near her tail. She was a mess.

"I'm sorry about Queenie," I said.

I thought it was impolite to drink right after making this remark.

"Are you OK?" she asked.

I knew she meant the episode with José. To everyone in Fresno who could read more than a menu, I was an item now, a thing to talk about. Somewhere someone was dunking a donut into a hot coffee and saying my name. Somewhere someone was saying, "See, I told you. He turned out *puro malo*."

"I'm OK, but it was lousy for José. His family is taking it hard." I almost added that José's family thought that it was my fault. My *nina* placed a hand on my shoulder and said, "Why don't you come with me?"

"To the pound?" I asked.

She nodded.

I hadn't seen my *nina* for about a year, and I was surprised that she had aged, too. Her eyes were also cloudy, and her hands shivered like leaves. Around her neck hung not one crucifix but three, a definite sign of age.

I agreed to go. I drank my Dr. Pepper, my only sweetness for the day, and carried Queenie to the car. My *nina* really cried now, letting out storm clouds from black mascara-ed eyes. Sludge flowed down her face as she petted Queenie and told her that God was going to watch over her.

It was a tough scene. As my *nina* drove, I petted

Queenie, feeling knobs of growth underneath her fur. Cancer? She whined when I pressed them, and I knew they were a bad sign.

"*Nina*," I said. "It's bad out there."

She knew what I meant.

We drove through a run-down part of Fresno, where young homies were ghosting on glue or paint or maybe angel dust. It was sad—no, frightening—all of them tripping like that. I checked out a clot of *cholitos* about Samuel's age. They were straddling bikes, their Dickies sawed off at the legs. Their hair was plastered down with hair nets, and around their throats our crucified Savior glinted on gold chains. Any one of them could have been the fool who stuck José. I wanted to ask my *nina* to pull over for a minute so I could kick their asses, but we had a stronger pull. We had to put down Queenie.

"Trash!" my *nina* growled at the *cholos*. "They ruined the town." Her knuckles whitened on the steering wheel. "I'm glad you didn't turn out like that."

"Me, too," I said in a near whisper.

We drove in silence, the city now becoming a rural landscape of ugly farms with rusting tractors sitting in the hot sun. I petted Queenie and my *nina* drove with her attention on the road. Finally she asked me a second time if I was OK, and I told her that I was. I told her life was pretty good and, lying big time, said that college was a lot of fun.

In the parking lot of the SPCA, my *nina* asked me to take Queenie in. I didn't know what to do. I petted Queenie, deaf and blind to our plans, and said, "You really want me to?"

My *nina*'s eyes were wet. Her profile was like Lincoln on a penny as she peered out the windshield, hands still on the steering wheel. I followed her gaze to a family who had come out of the SPCA, leading on a leash a youthful mutt with long, floppy legs.

"Here," my *nina* said, and sat up, pulling out her wallet. She handed me a twenty-dollar bill. "They're going to ask for a donation."

I couldn't face her or even Queenie, who shivered in my arms, eyes wet from inhaling her own onion. I stepped out of the car and closed the door quietly. I walked over the gravel that was as hot as coals. Before I went in, I looked back to the car, where my *nina* still sat with her hands on the steering wheel.

The smells inside the SPCA were strong, and the barking of dogs echoed in the hallway. I walked up to a foolish-looking white guy with thick glasses. He was scribbling on a clipboard, concentrating really hard. He didn't seem too bright.

"You taking that dog?" he asked, not raising his head.

He assumed that I had picked up Queenie from the back and was going to adopt her.

"Nah, homes," I said. "My dog's in bad shape."

The dude sized up Queenie, then me. "Is it a stray?" he asked.

"Family dog," I snapped. "You know, a pet. You ever hear of a family pet?"

The dude in glasses just stared at me.

"You better have your eyes checked, bro," I said. "I'm bringing in this dog to be put to sleep."

His mouth was just a line on his face. He handed me the clipboard, and I filled out a faded form. Since

I didn't know my *nina*'s address by heart, I wrote mine in.

"I'm sorry, Queenie," I whispered, and gave her one last hug, which squeezed a whimper from her throat. She didn't know me. She was blind and deaf. I could only press some of my love into her, this poor dog who did twelve years of living—a hundred or so years in dog life—and now was going to be put down.

The dude took her away, carefully because he could see that I was ready to burst with a sadness that bordered on anger. He was gone for about five minutes.

When he returned, I asked if there was a charge. He told me I could make a donation.

Right there I dug out the twenty dollars from my front pocket and—I felt bad, but I had to do it; I was starving and had to go on living—I said, "How's ten?"

"That's a twenty," the dude responded.

When the blue light near the ceiling zapped, I raised my eyes to the flash. Something got fried, and it might very well have been my soul. I said to the dude, "Yeah, I know it's a twenty. You got change?"

"Two tens?"

"Yeah, that's right," I said. "One ten for you and one for me."

With that the blue light fried another black-ass fly.

Lupe slapped Samuel on the arm, yanked his hair, and yelled that he should never, ever again pull a knife on a friend, meaning me.

After my *nina* had driven me back into town and fed me three sandwiches, which I washed down with an equal number of glasses of milk, and after I heard her tell me again and again that Queenie was such a good dog, and after adding my own two bits about how sweet Queenie was, I'd gone to see Lupe. He wasn't home. I'd returned the next day toward evening and told him that his asshole brother was messing up and if I had my way I was going to kick his ass. Now Lupe had Samuel cornered in the yard.

"You hear me? *¿Entiendes?*" Lupe growled. Lupe was scary when he got worked up. I knew he wouldn't last, though. I knew that one day some *vato* would hurt Lupe bad or he would slow down from scars and broken bones. But until then every hair on his body stood up when he got mad. And he got mad a lot.

"Say you're sorry!" Lupe scolded. He looked like G.I. Joe, legs spread and hands balled into fists. But instead of being miniature and green, Lupe was a hundred times taller and brown as the dirt at his feet.

To escape from Lupe, Samuel was running around their garden. The bottoms of his sneakers were bloody with tomatoes.

"Say you're sorry!" Lupe repeated. His finger was in Samuel's face. "Come on, *tonto*, spit it out! Say you're sorry, you sorry punk."

"I'm gonna get you," Samuel said through his tears. He was pointing at me, and while I knew I could choke him as easily as a burrito, I jumped just a bit. I thought of hurting him right there so that I wouldn't have to worry about him later. But I stayed calm. Lupe slapped him a few more times and told him go get run over in the street.

"I'm gonna get you, too," Samuel cried, pointing at Lupe.

"You better get on some weights first," Lupe muttered. He heaved an eggplant at Samuel, who took it on the back as he scaled the fence. I had to shake my head.

"I'm gonna get you, Eddie," Samuel cried from behind the fence. He threw a rock against the fence and trotted away.

Lupe got me a soda from his refrigerator, and we sat on his front lawn. I gave him the rundown on José Dominguez, right down to the blood that spilled in the shape of the United States. I even told him about Mr. Stiles's truck.

"Mala suerte," Lupe said.

I told him about the *mallate* who sold us onions. We had three sacks and if he wanted one, I could drag it over to his place. Luckily, he said no. Lucky because I hated the idea of dragging onions for two miles.

"You wanna go see José?" I asked.

Lupe thought about it, a stalk of grass in his mouth. "Yeah, why not?" he said, jumping to his feet and swatting the grass from his pants.

Since neither of us had a car, we started kicking down an alley in the direction of the community hospital. It was dusk, and the sun was going down, sailing west to work on the Chinese for a while. And since it was dusk, the valley wind whipped about, cooling off the asphalt and stirring up the stink of trash. In one alley we thought we saw Samuel tossing up burnt lightbulbs for the fun of it, but it was some other *mocoso*. The lightbulbs came down with an electric shatter that made the kids scream out of some crazy happiness. It was a great game when there was nothing to do.

82

"You ever been stuck?" Lupe asked.

"Nah, man," I said.

"It don't hurt. It's like ice."

When I looked at Lupe in disbelief, he pulled up his T-shirt and showed me a pinkish pucker of skin, like an extra belly button riding on his waist. "It's just like ice. They just stitch you and you're on your way. Just like Jack in the Box. You're in and out."

I didn't believe him. I had cut a finger on a hacksaw once and the skin opened like a gill, pouring out rich, sticky blood. It hurt. It hurt for days, and now at night in bed I could trace it with my thumb, a silken scar.

A cop's cruiser stopped at the end of the alley, stopped and eyed us, its windows glaring with leftover evening light. We walked past the cruiser and when I looked in, I saw a butch-haired cop. Behind those sunglasses I knew he was staring at our brown asses. He hated us because we were messing up the world.

Crazy Lupe gave the cop a stare, and when the door opened, he spread his arms out and with a jerk of his chin motioned, "¿Y qué?"

"You see two boys on bikes?" the cops asked. He was sounding us out, checking if our speech was slurred from sniffing. He wanted to know if he took his stick against our heads would he have to struggle or just pummel away because we were too messed up.

"No, sir," I said, then—I don't why—added, "we're off to the hospital. Really."

The cop checked us out, trying to assemble our *movida* as he studied and memorized our faces. He could have stopped us, but it was only a little after seven, not yet dark, and the night was going to get scary in about two hours. He probably figured why waste his time with a couple of young *burros* like us.

At the hospital there were still more people going in than going out. Lupe and I were smiling from ear to ear for the cool, cool air. We rode the elevator up to the fifth floor, where José shared a room with a cancer patient, a man who had made it into his seventies before fate caught up with him. As we tiptoed into the hospital room, thinking that maybe José was asleep, we saw that he was sitting up without any tubes hanging from his nose, talking with some dude.

"Hey, homes," Lupe crowed, friendlylike.

José, gray face and all, beamed. He was feeling better. But when the dude on the edge of the bed turned, I was shocked to see that it was Angel.

"Hey, Lupe," Angel said with a grin, and to me said, "*¡Flaco!* Where you been? Been looking for you, college boy."

"Don't call me that!"

Angel smiled, but behind that smile and his eyes, I could see his anger. He got off the bed and faced us, not wanting to take a chance that we might jump him right there. Angel was always careful, even with friends. Especially with the friends he kicked with.

"College sucks," I said to Angel. To José, I asked, "You feeling better?"

"A little better. I get out in three days," José said weakly. He told us that the homeboy who had stuck him missed his intestines by less than an inch. He held up his thumb and index finger, indicating an inch.

We crowed with José and told him over and over that we were sorry that he couldn't go over to Korea right away. We heard that the chicks were pretty nice.

"You're right, Eddie," José said. "This place is a hole. I ain't ever coming back."

"You gonna live in Korea?" Lupe asked.

"Maybe."

José cussed Fresno and all the *cholitos* ghosting in the streets. Lupe pulled up his shirt and showed José where he had been stuck. Angel bared his shoulder and showed us his wound, a little hook-shaped scar. I had nothing to show, except my knuckles where I caught a dude on his buck teeth.

"¡*Míra!*" José said. He showed us the plastic hospital bracelet with his name misspelled. It read JOES.

"It's close enough," Angel said. "It got all the letters."

"This is a sorry hospital," José said. He pointed to the next bed hidden behind a curtain and whispered, "That guy's gonna die."

Angel sneaked a peek and remarked, "He's got tubes in his nose." He touched his own nose and wiggled it. " 'Member when we used to do glue?"

"Don't bring it up," José said. He was a marine now and didn't want to hear about his past.

We talked sports and chicks for a while longer. At about eight o'clock I told José I had to go but would visit again.

"I'm sorry," I whispered in his ear. "I'm sorry that I caused you this trouble, bro."

He gripped my hand in friendship and said, "You didn't do nothing to me." He giggled and told me, "Don't forget, man, if a guy jumps you, just go for the throat."

I felt my throat. It had been sore for two days, but

now when I swallowed, spit went down; my windpipe was clear as a straw. I ran my palm over his marine haircut and said, "You're all messed up. Sleep it off."

I left the hospital alone. Lupe stayed, but I knew Angel would follow me, maybe a hundred feet behind or a block behind, a sneaky *ratoncito*. He would be on my case. He was going to try to kill me, and it wouldn't be with a knife but with my auntie's gun. I hid near some parked cars, waiting for Angel to trip out. After nearly an hour, I realized that Angel, the devil of all *cholos*, had sneaked out the back, through the same door where the dead bodies passed on their way to the mortuary.

CHAPTER 6

To lay open my heart with all its problems, I could have gone to a priest, some priest with pleats of wisdom on his brow. I could have knelt in one of those dank confessionals, squirmed, and mumbled, "Father, I have sinned." Or I could have gone to see a high school art teacher that I liked, except I heard he had moved to Oregon. There was my *nina* and then there was a cop I trusted. The cop was Raúl Hernandez, the older brother of Edgar, a guy I kicked with in high school. Raúl was a cop, but he had started an antigang program that mostly involved getting summer jobs for the homies. I would have loved one of those jobs except I wasn't bad enough. You had to be a real gangster to rake leaves, paint over *placas*, or pick up litter for good money.

Instead, on a Saturday morning I went to talk with Coach at Holmes playground, arriving just as he was opening up. The first kids, some barefoot and others wearing zoris that spanked the bottoms of their feet, ran to the rec room to check out four-square balls, tether balls, lopsided Ping-Pong balls, and, if they were dumb enough to shoot hoops in the sun, basketballs so plump with air that they dribbled themselves. The kids would work up a lather of sweat. After noon, when Coach opened up the pool, they would wash off that sweat swimming in the shallow water until closing time. I had gone through the same routine—hard play followed by a crocodile swim in our two-foot pool.

While Coach did his thing with the kids, I sat on top of a picnic table under a tree, feeling nervously guilty because early that morning I had taken the ten dollars meant for the SPCA and bought cereal and milk, Top Ramen, scarred plums at the farmers market, and two-for-one Bic razors. I hated myself for taking that money, cussed my own pathetic soul that cast a shadow no longer than a pissant. I prayed that Queenie, now probably incinerated, would forgive me.

It was late morning, and the sky, I noticed, was ribbed with high clouds. I thought of José. He was a good guy really, but his luck was no luck at all. He made one mistake: returning to Fresno on military leave. He should have gone to San Diego to drink beer. That way he could have poured himself onto the belly of an air cargo military plane and flown his brown ass to Korea for a tour of duty. He wouldn't be laid up in the hospital with a pair of landlocked seagulls circling outside.

Coach approached me with two sodas in one hand. He paused when he saw one of the kids, a trapeze artist, some future break-in artist for sure, climbing the backstop. Coach yelled for the kid to get down. The kid cussed loud enough for us to hear and dropped to the ground, raising dust around his shoes.

"What's going down, Eddie?" Coach asked. He handed me a Dr. Pepper, but before opening it, I explained the ABC's of my life, from my father's death to José's stabbing. This took all of ten minutes, including time-outs for Coach to yell at a couple of *mocosos* who were pressing their thumbs on the drinking fountain and squirting water. I rushed my story, which in my heart seemed complicated but when told seemed like the stuff you might read on one of those comic strips that come with Bazooka bubble gum.

I ended with, "I don't want to live here no more." I opened my soda and took a long swig. "It's ugly here."

Coach's face was a perpetual squint from years of scanning the playground. He squinted even in the dark shadows of the gym. He squinted because he was always busy figuring out what was going on around him. Were the kids putting their *placas* on the gym wall? Were the homies sniffing glue behind the backstop, or were men drinking beer in the sun-splintered bleachers? His radar was constantly on, and I imagined even in sleep his eyeballs moved behind their lids, checking things out.

"You really want to go away?" he asked me, though his attention was on two kids shouting at each other near the swings.

"I think so."

"You thought about maybe the service?"

I pictured José in his uniform, first standing straight as a birthday candle and then slumped over with two knife wounds.

"Not really," I said after a moment of silence.

Coach told me that he was in the army in Vietnam and it wasn't all bad. You met good people and bad people, and occasionally dead people. You got to see a little of the world, too. He had been to the Southeast and Japan, and almost got stationed in Germany. He said he got to go to college because of the service. Slapping my arm, he said, "Hey, man, I thought you was in college?"

"I told you I quit."

"You told me that?"

"Yeah, when I was here doing the lines for you."

Coach shook his head and remarked that he had lots to remember. He stood up like a shot and, hands cupped around his mouth, screamed for the two boys near the swings to knock it off. They had started shoving each other.

"Little gangsters," he muttered as he sat back down.

We sat in silence while we scanned the field together. From a distance I might have appeared to be his son, only a little taller and with no tattoos on my arms.

"I think the army could do you good," Coach said.

"I don't know, Coach," I said. I stared at my shoes, marked with grass stains and black and white spray paint from doing curbs. To test the coach, to find out how he felt, I muttered, "Angel is messing up."

"Angel," Coach said under his breath. Coach knew that Angel had caused bodies to bleed and old ladies to scream when they came home from shopping to find their houses broken into and ransacked. He'd known all of us glue sniffers—Angel, Lupe, dead Jesús, and me—since we were on bikes with training wheels. He'd known that most of us would mess up, some more than others. Still, it pained him. He muttered, "Angel, I'm gonna beat his ass one day."

90

I asked, "What should I do about Mr. Stiles? He still thinks that I stole his truck."

Coach winced and clicked his tongue. He said, "I'll call the man, Eddie," as he stood up from the bench and prodded me to the rec room, his arm around me, assuring me that everything would be sweet as *pan dulce.* He was wiser than a priest and kinder than my art teacher. He was as clever as the cop who had started the gang program.

"You sure you should call him?" I asked nervously.

"Sure I'm sure."

As Coach dialed on an old funky rotary telephone, I asked, "What are you going to tell him?"

"The truth, Eddie. What else can I say?" Coach swigged from his soda and squinted when he got someone on the line, a habit that would crease his face until he resembled a paper bag.

"Mr. Stiles," he started, hopping onto a stool. He introduced himself as head coach at Holmes playground and proceeded to sing a song of my saintly goodness, so strongly that I wanted to get to know the guy he was talking about. He even told Mr. Stiles about my playground years, bringing up the time when I was crafts champion in the lanyard division and runner-up in the plaster-of-paris division with a perfect replica of George Washington's head. Coach crowed "Yeah, I'm sure" three times—a good sign, I figured. He was pulling for me. He pressed the phone against his chest. "I got to talk to him alone. Go outside for a sec."

I did as I was told, wanting to live up to Coach's description of me as a dude who followed orders. I went outside, almost skipping in the hopscotch painted on the cement. While I stood shaded under the overhang of the rec room, I finished the last sweet drops of my Dr. Pepper. I turned and saw Coach in the window. He was nodding his head, jabbering. At that moment I heard my name called, and not nicely.

"Eddie, you ain't shit!"

Samuel was standing twenty feet in front of me with two of his homeboys, one wearing his mama's hair net. I checked their mouths to see if they had been inhaling spray paint. They were clean, thus sober, thus dangerous.

"What do you want, man?"

Samuel showed me his blade.

"You trying to scare me, *tonto*?" I asked. My hands closed into fists. Out of the corner of my eye I could see the trash can, which I thought I could hide behind and then use to make him bleed if he tried to stick me.

"You're scared, huh? Think you're all *bravo*!"

"In your dreams, little gangster."

Samuel sent a stream of spit near my feet.

"How come you're drooling?" I asked with a snicker.

He spit again and growled, "Me and Angel are going to get you, man."

So. So little Samuel, *diablito*, was kicking with Angel.

"Where's Angel?"

"Forget you, man!"

"Does your brother know you're with Angel?"

Samuel moved toward me, and I jumped behind the garbage can. I took the latch into my hands and heaved it up, shoulder high, ready to come down on Samuel's head if he came any closer.

"You look like a garbage man." One of Samuel's friends laughed.

"Yeah, man," I said with a huff in my breath. "And you're the garbage!"

From the rec room, the telephone still to his ear, Coach sized up the scene and whacked the window with his palm. The moist outline of his palm stayed for a second and then slowly evaporated. Coach moved his mouth, trying to scare Samuel. Samuel gave him the finger, not in the least scared or respectful because Coach had been the man who taught him how to swing on the swing, slide down the slide, and swim in the swimming pool when he was just out of diapers.

"I'm gonna get you, man," Samuel said to me when he saw Coach put down the telephone, preparing to chase Samuel off the playground.

The three *cholitos* ran off, none of them looking back until they were in the parking lot. They gave us, Coach and me, the finger, their gestures going up and down like the devil's pitchfork. They disappeared in the vapor of heat beginning to bear down on Fresno.

Without a word, Coach returned to the rec room and spoke to Mr. Stiles some more. But when he got off the telephone, Coach called Samuel a bunch of names, and he was so worked up that he opened the soda machine again and brought out two more sodas.

"That little punk," Coach scolded.

"He ain't that bad," I said. It felt strange sticking up for Samuel, and I didn't know why I said it except that I wanted to calm Coach down.

Coach swallowed a healthy swallow and, clapping his hands together, said, "Mr. Stiles wants to hire you back."

I pictured myself on the little hill with the birch tree. My eyelashes were batting dirt.

"Hire me back?"

"He says that you work good."

I pictured the rise and fall of my hoe and then the little kid on the tricycle patrolling the streets.

"Everything's going to be smooth, bro."

Coach swigged on his soda, his Adam's apple jumping up and down. He burped. He looked in the telephone book, all the time asking if I wanted to join the marines, army, navy, or what.

"I don't know, Coach." I was suddenly scared. I wanted to get out of Fresno, but at the same time it alarmed me. I was nineteen and I hadn't been anywhere—two times to L.A. and four times to Sacramento. But Sacramento didn't count. It looked a lot like Fresno.

"Pick one, Eddie."

I told him the navy because I liked water.

"Good choice!" he boomed. He looked up the number of the navy recruiting center, dialed, and immediately got a recruiter. Coach started in again, a real salesman. "Hey, I'm the coach over at Holmes playground . . . nah, not homes—Holmes!" Smiling, he said, "Yeah, yeah."

I left the rec room, but this time I didn't feel like playing hopscotch. My legs seemed heavy, like those bags of onions the *mallate* had sold me and José. I moved slowly toward the baseball diamond. The glare hurt my eyes. I wandered over to the picnic bench and would have sat down except the sun was blazing there. Joining the navy actually scared me. All the guys I knew from high school chose the marines or the army. I wondered if you had to know how to swim really good or if they would teach you. I had almost drowned once when me and a bunch of other *cholitos* went swimming in a motel pool. With the ocean a million times larger, I wondered if I had a chance.

"Hey," Coach yelled, waving for me to come back.

I walked back to the rec room as if I were slogging waist deep in water. And hot water, I figured.

After another *hombre a hombre* talk with Coach, I trudged home under the hot sun, soaped and washed my armpits, and changed into a fresh T-shirt with the Fresno State bulldog growling on the front. I planned to appear patriotic, if not an outright cheerleader for American sports. I wanted to resemble a straight-ahead kind of dude, someone who had his act together.

The recruiting office was located downtown on the Fresno Mall. There were winos and homeless people to step over. When I got there, it was four o'clock. I was grateful for cool air. On the wall hung a poster of a nuclear sub crashing in water. Another had a bad-ass fighter jet taking off from an aircraft carrier. There were three kinds of flags, splashy brochures, and a portrait of our president smiling. As I walked around sizing up the place, the president's eyes followed me. His smile seemed to deepen, get bigger. At any moment a pair of fangs would show.

In the corner there was a water cooler. Since no

one greeted me, I tiptoed over there, pulled down a paper cup, and filled it.

"Don't bubble," I said to the water cooler. But it did. It bubbled and burped. Right away a recruiter came out of a cubicle, wiping his hands on a tiny paper napkin. He had been eating back there.

"Hello," he said in a husky voice, as if his ancestors were bullfrogs. He was about forty, I guessed, and his skin was leathery. Maybe it got that way from staying in the salt spray for years.

He told me his name and I told him mine. He waved a hand at the mascot on my T-shirt and said, "Tarkanian is going to turn the dogs around." Jerry Tarkanian was a second-year basketball coach, the one who for years bit on a towel in front of Las Vegas TV cameras. Now he was biting on a towel for Fresno cameras.

I drank from my paper cupful of water. I was nervous. Should I have my birth certificate, high school diploma, library card?

"I'm interested in maybe joining up?" I tried to look tall.

The recruiter's eyes narrowed, just slightly, as if he was an eagle and I was a thirsty gopher seen from above. He told me to sit down and I did, scooting out a chair in front of his desk, which sported a model clipper ship and an aircraft carrier. There were also two telephones, one black and one white, a curious combination.

"Did you graduate?" he asked in his bullfrog voice. There was a single row of ribbons on his chest and a couple of buffed medals.

"You mean high school?"

He nodded and reached for a clipboard with a Bic pen dangling from a greasy string. He made the clip yawn open and pushed in a blank form.

"Yeah," I said. I told him that I had pretty good grades and ran track.

"Tell me more about yourself," he prompted as he leaned back in his chair. He reminded me of my elementary school principal.

For the second time that day, I explained my life, from my father's death to José's stabbing, this time taking a little longer because I stopped to tell him that in my freshman year I had almost won state championship in the five-mile run except I had worn cheap shoes. I expected him to smile. I expected him to slap his hands together and crow, "You almost won state?"

He wet his lips and asked if I was a citizen of this country, not Mexico, and I told him that I was. I added, "My mom lives in Merced."

"You like girls?" he asked, pushing along and half listening to me.

"Like everybody else." Norma's breasts appeared and disappeared in a blink on the back of my retinas.

"You got a girl now? You married?" He leaned forward in his chair. "You the father of any kids?"

I wagged my head.

"I got kids," he crowed. "Five. Kids are wonderful." He named them off, all of them names that began with the letter *D*: Diane, Darrell (named after him), Dale, Donna, and Danny.

He bragged that they were good kids, and I listened with my hands on my lap. Then it was my turn to talk. I told him I wanted to join the service because I wanted to travel. I told him I wanted to see icebergs and whales and penguins and whatever. I guess he had heard this before because he didn't have much to say except, "I like your ambition."

When I started to complete the form, which was three pages long, the recruiter, whom I was liking less and less, disappeared into a side cubicle. I heard him chomping potato chips. I figured they were barbecue-flavored. The chomping stopped when the front door opened. In came a dude I knew from high school, Larry something, a real stoner, a heavy-metal freak. Dripping sweat, his face as pink as a crab in boiling water, he wore a Rolling Stones T-shirt with a big red tongue lapping out over the front.

"Oh no," I muttered to myself. I felt depressed at the thought he and I were in the same place in life— desperate to get out the easy way, the service. No, we're not equals, I thought. I'm better than that clown!

Larry looked around, wrinkling his nose as he picked up the scent of barbecue potato chips. He walked slowly toward me, but when he saw the water cooler he aimed for it. He drank three cups, belching in a disgusting way. Refreshed, he said "Hey" to me.

Barely looking up at him, I said, "Hey, dude," and kept on filling out the form. I was embarrassed to be seated in the navy recruiting office, worrying about how to spell *deceased*.

"Hello, young man," the recruiter boomed as he came out of the cubicle smelling of barbecue chips.

Larry stuttered but managed to tell the recruiter that he was interested in the navy. Larry rattled on about how his uncle was in the navy during Vietnam and how great it was.

"Have a seat," the recruiter said to Larry. To me, he asked, "How's it going?"

I told him OK. I told him I was filling out the form but I was still undecided about joining. I wanted to consider the army as well. The recruiter hitched up his pants and got heavy. He told me I could go into computers, maybe radar or missiles. He asked if I could stand blood, and I shrugged my shoulders.

"Well, there's nursing, too."

I pictured José on the sidewalk with blood flowing like Pepsi from a bottle.

He said I could get assigned to an aircraft carrier. Right then the water cooler burped on its own. "Or a submarine."

"I don't know how to swim good," I remarked. I stood up.

"The navy isn't about swimming," his voice boomed. "It's about being a man!"

"I thought that was the marines."

"Forget the marines! The navy is far more intelligent. We got timing! You ever see a fighter jet take off from a carrier?"

I shook my head.

"It's beautiful because it's all a matter of timing." He wet his lips. "You like computers, don't you?"

"I guess." I had started to creep toward the door.

"You ever save anyone's life?" he asked. The faint smell of barbecue chips still clung to the air.

"Not really." I was almost at the door. The telephone, the white one I think, began to ring loud as a siren. I explained to the recruiter that this was a big decision and I couldn't rush it. I needed to talk with my mother.

"How much you weigh?" He was nearly on top of me.

"I don't know," I stammered. "One fifty?"

"Perfect! You can work rescue. You like helicopters?"

"Yeah, well..." I stuttered like a fool, like Larry, who had taken the model carrier in his hands and was examining it. He had the IQ of a kid who plays with boats in the bathtub.

The recruiter stood in the doorway with his hands on his hips and told me that the navy was better than the army any day. I scooted out of there, sweatier from this air-conditioned encounter than from the heat outside. I bought a *raspada*, shaggy with coconut, from a Mexican *vendedora* working the mall. Returning to my apartment, I stepped over winos, the homeless, and stray dogs with ladders of ribs poking through. Hunger, I saw, was crawling from one end of the street to the other.

Sunday. I woke early, mad because Mom still hadn't sent the money order for twenty dollars. It wasn't that much, I figured. I tried to call her and yell at her for being cheap, but my phone was dead.

I dressed, ate two bowls of cereal, and took the bus to Mr. Stiles's house. On Saturday evening when my phone was still alive, Mr. Stiles and I had talked. He had forgiven me, he said, after Coach called him, and now he needed my help again. Weeds were coming up in all the flower beds. The window screens were hollering to be washed. Holes had to be dug for two new fruit trees, a peach and an apricot. He needed me, and I was grateful.

It was early morning, so the bus I rode was nearly empty. We went north toward the newer houses, where it was Fresno yet not Fresno. It was another place altogether, foreign and scrubbed. I felt like I was walking inside the pages of *Sunset* magazine. It was pretty cool, yet scary. Everyone was blond.

I got off, thanking the bus driver, a large black woman. I walked the mile from the bus stop and passed the house where the old man had hired me to move the air conditioner. His house was quiet, the front dark as sunglasses.

On another street, I checked out the curb where I had painted some numbers. The Fresno sun had baked them in permanently.

A car drove by, filled with people on their way to church. They glared at me, all of them probably thinking: That homeboy is going to break into our house!

As I approached Mr. Stiles's house, I saw his red Toyota truck parked at the corner. It was bright, recently washed, so glossy that flies would slide off the hood. I circled it, looking for dents. But it was smooth. I was glad the homies hadn't messed it up.

I didn't have to knock on Mr. Stiles's door. He was in the garage, wearing safety goggles, sawing planks the length of a coffin.

"Eddie," he said.

We shook hands. I told him how sorry I was about his truck. "I wouldn't steal from you," I nearly blubbered. I was glad to be trusted. I felt that I would slave for this man, work until there was nothing left in my shoulders and back. Blisters would rise from my palms and my fingernails would crust with dirt. I glanced around the garage, searching for the shovel. "What do you want me to do, Mr. Stiles?"

His hand squeezed my shoulder. "Relax."

He went inside the house by way of the door in the garage and was gone for a few minutes. I noticed my bike, which was propped in the corner, a lazy spiderweb in the front spokes. When he returned, he was holding up two icy sodas.

"Which would you like?"

He held up a Dr. Pepper and a Diet Pepsi. I chose the Dr. Pepper.

"Eddie," he started nervously.

"Mr. Stiles?"

He wanted to tell me something, but he squeezed my shoulder and led me out to the backyard. He pointed vaguely and told me to dig a hole.

"Right here?" I kicked the ground with my toe.

"Perfect."

"An orange tree?"

"I think so."

I looked around the backyard, which had a sod lawn but was still unfinished. A wheelbarrow held sacks of cement and bricks that were going to become a patio.

"Where's your wife, Mr. Stiles?" I asked.

He told me she was at church with their two children. He grimaced. "Eddie...," he faltered.

"What? Did I do something wrong?"

His blue eyes swam in moisture. His body gave off the aura of Aqua Velva. "Nah, you didn't do anything wrong." He turned and stomped off toward the garage.

I put on a pair of cotton gloves and fetched the shovel leaning against the side of the house. There's no time to lose, I told myself. Let's get to work. I was redeemed by the trust of a man who had once thought I had done him wrong.

Mr. Stiles disappeared, and I shoveled with fury, as if I hated the hard, compacted dirt, and soon my back was as wet as a washcloth. I stopped, breathing hard. I wiped my brow, the sweat stinging my eyes. I bent down and pulled up roots. I gathered pieces of broken bottle, blue with age. Feeling good, I hummed like a bee.

I drained the rest of my soda and shoveled for fifteen minutes straight. The hole got wider and deeper and I stepped in it, measuring its depth. It was nearly knee-deep. I felt like I was getting somewhere and then felt something under my shoe like a baseball. I got out of the hole and, dropping to my knees, I clawed it out. It was a bulb of some kind, onionlike. I peeled off a sheet of its skin and sniffed it. It smelled only of earth.

I continued shoveling, pleased with my progress but wishing I had a Walkman to listen to. I sang and stopped singing. I rested, leaning on my shovel. As I raked my hand across my brow, protecting my eyes from salty sweat, a guy jumped over the fence. For one eerie moment I thought he was a sailor, that the recruiter had sent this man out to haul me back. Then I saw two guys come running out of the garage. The entire navy was showing up! They hustled toward me and as they reached for their waists, I muttered to myself, "No, Mr. Stiles! You didn't." I let go of the shovel and raised my hands.

"Police," they sang like a choir.

They had me facedown on the dirt, handcuffing me. They yanked me to my feet, read me my rights, and pushed me toward the garage. I walked with my head down, throat tight around a lump of big-time sorrow. I spotted my bike in the corner and thought how close I'd been to getting it back. Now this, the police hauling this homie away. If I ever got my bike back, it would be smothered in spiderwebs.

I was led from the garage to an idling cruiser. Neighbors were on lawns, shading their eyes and assessing the story. I heard someone ask, "Did he try to break into the Stiles's house?"

"What did I do?" I asked the cops at each side of me.

The cop said that I was wanted for the brutal beating of an old man in a Laundromat.

"I never hurt anybody," I cried. "I wash my dirty clothes at home. I don't *use* no Laundromat!"

It didn't do any good. The cop with a black crayon of a mustache pushed me in the back of the cruiser and slammed the door. He got in, his side of the car rocking under his weight. He checked in with the central office. He was on his way, he informed the dispatcher, and I told him that I had never been to a Laundromat but once. I told him that I never stole or hurt anyone unless they asked for it. The cop told me to shut up.

The cruiser pulled away and when I peered out the window, I saw the kid on the trike racing along, trying to keep up.

CHAPTER 7

After two hours of on-and-off questioning by detectives who smelled of hamburgers and hate, I was released on that same Sunday afternoon, just as all the major-league ball games were being tallied across America. The scores were what I first heard of the outside world when I stepped outside into the warm afternoon. Near the entrance to the police station, a blind man was sitting on a folding chair, listening to a transistor radio and selling gum, candy bars, and cigarettes. I bought two Snickers bars from the blind man, who was wearing country overalls. He gave off the scent of tobacco and there were at least three crucifixes hanging around his large neck. He was really into Jesus, needed Him, I guess, because any *cholo* could rip the poor guy off without his noticing. Then I saw he had a smooth wooden ax handle to bring down on some thief's fingers. Perfect protection, I thought. Christ and a club!

I took my two Snickers to a bench in front of the police department, which was kind enough to provide places for criminals to sit and smoke cigarettes. A squirrel from one of the sycamore trees climbed down and begged. I stomped my foot and told the greedy beast to scram. My problems fit together like a set of

Legos: Mr. Stiles's truck had been used in the robbery of a Laundromat in Kerman, a town outside Fresno. The thieves, homies from all descriptions, beat up an old dude. The cops thought I was connected, and even Mr. Stiles had his suspicions. I told the detectives over and over that the Toyota pickup had gotten gaffled in front of my apartment. I was no thief, I cried, and never got into hurting anyone unless the asshole started it.

They did a computer search, I'm sure, but whether they came up with the ancient history of my scrawling *placas* in wet cement, I don't know. They didn't book me, or even fingerprint me or take my picture. They said these were "conferences" and I had a right to a lawyer and all that, but if we could talk for a while, matters could be settled. And they were. They let me go. I sounded confused as I explained my life for the third time in two days. I even confessed about Queenie, admitting I snagged ten dollars. My throat went dry on this admission, but the cops turned away when I expressed with a lot of heart how sorry I was for Queenie and my *nina*. I didn't know if they were smirking or holding themselves back from pummeling me for being a lowlife.

I knew Coach was not to blame, and maybe not even Mr. Stiles, who must have turned me in. Still, I felt sorry for myself. Even my mom hadn't sent me the twenty dollars I'd asked for. When the squirrel returned to beg with its tiny outstretched paws, I stomped my foot and told him to go play in the street.

The rush of sugar from the candy bars perked me up. I noticed there were more people going into the police station than leaving. Since I was downtown near the hospital, in fact in sight of its smokestack poking between trees, I decided to hike over and see José if he was still there. I got up with a grunt, bone tired but ready to move on. I had to get out of view of the police and the nasty squirrel that couldn't take no for an answer.

I walked the three blocks to the hospital, and before visiting José, I ventured into the rest room. I looked like a tortured refugee. My hair was a nest of powdery dirt. My face was smudged, and the black under my fingernails suggested I had clawed my way out of a hole. And maybe I had. The cops had let me go.

I rode the elevator to the fifth floor, but when I sauntered into José's room, I discovered he was gone. In his bed sat a gray-haired woman with tubes in her nose and arms. I backed out of the room.

"Nurse," I called to the first person I saw in a white uniform, an immense woman who came up the hallway pushing a laundry cart. "My friend José is...," I stammered. But she kept rolling her laundry cart and told me, "Check at the counter."

I took her suggestion, but not before I scared myself by thinking that José was dead and the second-year mortuary students could be working on his body at that very moment. I was panting when I asked the woman at the counter. She punched in numbers on her computer. "Released to his family," she told me, and turned to a blinking telephone.

We've both been released, I thought as I left the hospital and started toward my apartment. The evening was coming down with its curtain of dark, moist air. Orange porch lights were glowing. Some kids were getting in the last few licks of front-yard baseball. I walked briskly, and when I heard a gunshot in the distance and a couple arguing, their voices full of slurs from drinking, I was aware I was getting closer to southeast Fresno.

At my apartment I was surprised to see my bike leaning against the wall near my door. Although I was as thirsty as the lawn and a six-pack of 7UP was sitting in the wire basket, I didn't reach for it. I stepped back, suspecting a trap.

"Mr. Stiles," I called.

The neighbor's wind chime sounded.

"Mr. Stiles," I called louder.

A truck passed in the street, one headlight gone.

I stood in the driveway of our duplex. I hesitated, like that squirrel, but then slowly approached my bike. In the gleam of my neighbor's porch light, I saw a note standing up in the six-pack. I unrolled it and discovered a clean ten-dollar bill. The note read: "Eddie, I'm sorry about the police, but I had to be sure that you were not involved in the assault on that poor Filipino man. God bless you. You work very hard." The note was unsigned.

I felt like crying. I sat on the steps for a few moments. My eyes were raw, my soul trampled by bad luck and bad luck's brother, hard times.

I hauled my bike into the house and threw open the windows. I put the six-pack of 7UP into the freezer. I showered and turned on the TV. When I thought the sodas were cold enough, I brought them out and drank three, one right after another. That night I tossed in my sleep.

I stayed in my apartment for two days watching

television and listening to the radio. I went out only when I had eaten all my cereal, eggs, and Top Ramen. With the ten dollars from Mr. Stiles, I bought groceries at an overpriced Korean mom-and-pop store, throwing caution to the wind and buying a carton of Neapolitan ice cream. I ate half of it when I got home, not even bothering to put it in a bowl. I dug in with a serving spoon. I thought about the police, how they had picked me up and let me go. Were they bored with me? Bored with all of us homies and ex-homies? I knew a lot of dudes who got picked up by cops. Some deserved it, but for others it was just a case of *mala suerte*. In those two days I wavered between hate for Mr. Stiles to something like love for him because he was the kind of guy who was putting together a life for his family. I still couldn't make up my mind.

During those two days alone, I paced the room as if I were in an asylum and I declared war on a family of cockroaches long as jalapeños. Since I hadn't spent much time in my apartment during the past two weeks, those freeloaders had moved in, thinking no one cared about the place. They didn't seem to care that there was nothing to eat. They came out from under the refrigerator to draw fresh air. Like tourists, they checked out the kitchen sink, the bathroom sink, the dining table, the dead telephone, even my arm when I was sitting on the couch watching television. They raced around the lips of glasses and cereal bowls, which made me wash the dishes all over again. I was full of hate and disgust for those cockroaches. But I had my laugh when they slipped into the toilet bowl. They crawled the face of the refrigerator, and when they grew still, they were like the cute magnets that hold doctor bills and coupons. But I declared war on them. When I'd finished my ice cream, I set the carton on the floor and hid around the corner, on all fours, waiting for them to sniff out the sugary scent. And they came in pairs, like the animals on Noah's ark. When I thought I had enough of them in there, their tiny legs sticky from the ice cream, I stomped back into the kitchen and closed the hatch on them. I rattled the carton like a *maraca* Outside, I stomped on the carton and threw it into the garbage. I spotted a boy in the alley and when he asked what I was doing, I told him I was cleaning up. He was holding a softball with a flap of skin ready to fall off.

"You want to play catch?" I asked.

I played catch with the boy, a *gordito* whose belly showed under his smallish T-shirt. I felt sorry for him because, of the hundred times I tossed the ball to him, sometimes even underhand, he only caught six or seven cleanly. About an hour later when I entered my apartment, I was surprised to see that the cockroaches had returned. Their antennae were all bent, and some of their legs were crippled, but they were eager as ever. They were the same ones. At that point I let the homies settle in.

Wednesday morning, when I was going through a tooth-grinding hate for Mr. Stiles, a fist pounded my front door. Immediately I thought, Angel. I reached for the bat set by the couch, choked it, and muttered, "Angel, I'm going to mess you up." When I threw open the door I was facing José, yellow as a tulip and leaning on a cane. He was wearing a T-shirt and nicely pressed khakis. He didn't grab me by the throat, either. He didn't use his marine tactics.

"Hey, Eddie," he said weakly. He chuckled, "I'm going to make it." He chuckled some more and asked politely for me not to touch him because the stitches hurt like hell.

I glanced over his shoulder. Coach was coming up the driveway, head down and muttering to himself. He had his regular playground scowl pleated all over his face.

"How you feeling, dude?" I asked José. "Come on in. Don't step on the cockroaches."

"What?"

"My new homies." I didn't bother to explain as he hobbled in on his cane. "What's going on?"

We were going fishing, that's what was going on. Coach came up the steps, calling, "Eddie, Eddie, Eddie!" He gave me *un abrazo* and said that he was really sorry that Mr. Stiles had set me up. He hadn't heard what happened until yesterday, and yesterday was a tough one at the playground: a minor gang fight between Hmongs and Mexicans, and a major theft that would leave everyone dry—some *vatos* had hauled off the soda machine during the night.

Coach had known most of us when we were knee-high gangsters with candy cigarettes hanging from our mouths. We whipped ourselves with Red Whips and sucker punched each other for gum and grimy quarters. We were playground kids. He knew our problems, which were his not long ago. He knew that we needed fresh air and distance from the little shop of horrors we created for ourselves. I could see this as he scanned my glamorous apartment, where the only beauty was a couple of babes from the annual swimsuit issue of *Sports Illustrated*.

So we locked up. We got into Coach's baby blue Ford Pinto, bought burgers and fries, and hauled out of town, heading east toward Centerville, where Coach said there was a little creek, his secret, that was slippery with fish, mostly bluegill and some trout. We ate our food and turned up the car radio, its cracked speakers creating new versions of songs we already knew.

We passed mile after hot mile of grape vineyards, orange and lemon groves, and pastures where horses stood lazily in the sun, swatting themselves with their tails. From behind barbed wire, cows chewed grass that hung like beards from their mouths.

"I like the country," I said from the backseat, where I held on to the tackle and jugs of water. I liked mountains and lakes mostly, and in spring I liked the blossoms that made you sneeze every few minutes. But four-legged animals scared me. I didn't suffer from that fear with friends around, though. There were three of us, and I was the skinniest. I would be the last to be eaten.

"It didn't work out with the navy?" Coach asked. He raised his eyebrows in the rearview mirror.

"You were going to join the navy?" José asked in a surprised voice. Careful not to pull his stitches, he turned to hear me over the radio. I told him I had visited the recruiter and filled out some forms, but I was still going to think about my decision. José said, "If I had to do it a second time, I'd join the navy."

"Guess what," I said over the noise of the radio and wind from the window.

"What?" both of them asked.

"You don't have to know how to swim."

"You're bullshitting us," José said with a smile on his face.

"It's the truth."

"What if you drown?" José asked. "You think of that?"

"Well, it's your problem. All I'm saying is that you don't got to know how to swim."

They pondered that notion for the next three miles, while the countryside flashed by and bugs of every type splattered against the windshield. We stopped to buy a can of worms at a rickety mom-and-pop. I liked the place. Dusty sunlight fell from the window. The owner's dog lay on a worn rug. The floor was wood, and there were photographs of dudes holding up their catches. In one photo, a guy was holding a fish nearly as tall as he was. He looked short, but still, a fish as tall as you, and a picture to prove it!

Coach asked the clerk if there had been any fires yet. In the foothills the yellowish grasses seemed ready to go up under the kick of heels or the glint of car mirrors. The hills burned often. Fire ate with a great hunger until nothing was left but a burnt scent in the air. Even the poor rabbits and gophers got scorched.

"Nah," the clerk growled. "Ain't seen no fire yet. Give it a month and some city fool will start one." He wet his lips. "You from the city?"

The three of us nodded like yokels.

"I don't mean you men necessarily," the clerk said, changing his tune.

We told him we understood, and that none of us smoked, drank, or cussed.

We drove to Coach's secret creek, which was no

secret at all because most of the high school students knew the place. They drank there, talked about the names of girls that they'd like to tattoo on their arms, and peed into that river while looking up at the stars. It was the place to be when you were seventeen.

I had gone there one fall when leaves had burned golden and the sky was blue as an eye. I borrowed my mom's car and I drove Sylvia Hernandez there. It was early afternoon. We skimmed rocks over the water and smiled from ear to ear because it was something like love, something like a scene from a movie. Voices from fishermen floated over the water. Ducks honked. Birds scrambled along the sand, searching. I didn't kiss her or hold her hand, even when we sat in the car and she took my keys and placed them at the opening of her skirt. She teased me sweetly. We smiled until we hurt.

"Yeah, we been here before," José said as Coach maneuvered the car over the ruts.

Secret or not, we parked near the river and got out of the car, a huge cloud of dust stirring about us. We waved at the dust and coughed as we unloaded the car. We assembled our fishing poles and took an army blanket to the river's edge, where we sat with socks and shoes off, our toes wiggling like the worms in the can. Mosquitoes found us immediately, and a whole nation of gnats. I didn't care. As long as some wolf didn't come jumping out of the knee-high weeds and snap my head off, I could live with the little pests.

"It's nice," Coach said.

The green river flowed cool as mint and made us think that we were moving, going places. I watched the water and my pole with its fishing line as thin as a spiderweb. The river surged over a few rocks jutting from the water. Birds skimmed the water recklessly, and now and then a toad the color of mud flopped along the reedy banks.

"It's real nice," José said.

I asked José when his stitches were coming out, and he said in a day or two. He slowly, maybe painfully, peeled off his shirt and showed us a body that was pale but still marine-hard. The stitches on his shoulder were as black as mascara, but the ones on his waist were clean and pale. The pale ones would dissolve on their own, he explained, and the others would have to be pulled.

I hesitated but had to ask, "Does it feel like ice when you get cut?"

Coach didn't stop José from answering. He was curious, too.

"I don't know, bro," José said. "Kinda."

"I'm sorry," I told José. I felt that I was to blame because of Mr. Stiles's truck.

José shrugged and sighed at the river that surged over rocks and driftwood like time itelf.

"You didn't see their faces?" I asked.

"Yeah, I saw them."

Coach and I looked at each other. We waited for him to offer us a fuller explanation, waited for him to finish tossing a few flat rocks into the water.

"Well?" Coach asked.

"You mean, did I know the dudes?" José asked. He smacked a mosquito on his shoulder. He brought away his palm and shook off the flattened insect.

Then he answered, "Nah, I didn't know them." His attention was now diverted to the water, and his stare was far away, maybe to that day when he got stuck and lay on the sidewalk. Maybe he was reliving the moment the knife entered and exited. After a while he added, "Just lowlife homies like the ones you and me and Eddie know."

Coach rolled a stick between his palms. "I know you guys have it hard."

"*Hard* ain't the word, Coach," José responded. "I come back for two days and a homie stabs me. Messed me up!" He bit his lip. I thought he might start crying.

I started talking a boatload of nonsense. I announced to José and Coach that I was going back to college next fall. My smile was lopsided as a pumpkin's when I said this. I bragged to them about learning a lot in air-conditioning. Neither of them believed me; they lowered their gaze to the sand at their feet. Still, I continued enlightening them about thermostats, ducts, Freon, union wages, and the helicopters used to bring in heavy-duty air-conditioning units. I informed them that air-conditioning in cars didn't use that much gas, just a little more than if you had your windows rolled down. I grinned. I tried to look all excited over this nonsense. I told them about a unit that fell six floors through the roof and right on top of someone's foot on the first floor.

"Eddie," Coach whispered. He winced at me, tender but direct. "Be quiet, man."

We sat in silence while the gnats and mosquitoes circled us, loving our heat and blood. Then Coach jumped up, slapped his palms together, and yelled to me, "Come on! Take your clothes off!" He peeled off his T-shirt. I was surprised to see a tattoo that said THE GOOD SHEPHERD on his back. I wanted to ask about the tattoo, and so did José, who was admiring it with his mouth hanging open. Jesus our Savior had always been big in our lives. On Coach's back, he seemed even bigger. But neither of us said anything.

"You mean, get in the water?" I asked, already on my feet and considering if I should do it. I stripped off my shirt, then my pants. I stood in my *chones*, my underwear. Coach was naked. But not far away there was a parked car with one door flung open. And a while ago we saw some kids on dirt bikes riding the dusty trail. Coach didn't seem to care, but I did! I left my underwear on and followed him, stepping lightly on the rocks.

"It's cold," I screamed.

"It ain't cold," Coach argued. "It's just that you're hot."

That sort of made sense. The river ran between my legs as I slowly entered it. I took the icy cold like a homie and asked Coach if he remembered teaching us how to swim.

"You know how to swim good?" His voice vibrated from the cold.

"A little bit. Dog paddle. You know, float."

And that's what I did. I floated like a toy duck on water. I thought, Maybe the navy's not such a bad idea. Water seemed a part of me. I dunked my head. I envisioned myself from the bank where José was watching, envisioned myself floating with my head on the water and my body down below with the fish.

117

Coach screamed, "Don't drown, Eddie." He was hugging himself, shivering.

But I floated almost peacefully, my feet touching bottom so that I wasn't scared. I floated downstream, the sun gold as a ring and the sky like heaven itself. I dunked my head again and my ears hurt.

I rode the current, and when I thought I had gone too far, I paddled to the bank. Then over rocks, spindly leaves, and driftwood, I cut a path back, my *chones* heavy with sand and water. I shook the sand from my underwear and examined my private parts, now shriveled to a thumb and two walnuts but gleaming with gold silt. Gold or no gold, I was embarrassed for myself. I was just too small.

That afternoon the fish nibbled on our bait but wouldn't bite. We couldn't blame them. On a blanket, we talked about sports and fights we had gotten into and out of, and brayed like donkeys about girls who were foolish enough to like us. We described the scariest and bloodiest movies we had ever seen, even acting out some of the parts. And each of us had our favorite rockers. Coach said over and over that the greatest rock group since the beginning of Chicano time—the 1960s—was Malo. José and I shook our heads. "Never heard of of them, Coach." He seemed hurt. His look was comical, like a boy who'd been told to go to his room. He just couldn't understand that we had never heard of them.

José asked about the tattoo on Coach's back. Coach was sitting on the bank, pouring sand through his hands like an hourglass. He said he got it inked before he went to 'Nam, that he wished he hadn't gotten it but there it was, on his back, forever. Even in death, he said. He advised us against tattoos. José smiled. Rolling carefully onto his stomach, he jiggled his pants down and showed us two spiders on his pale butt.

"That's ugly," I said.

"You're jealous, homes." He laughed, his *nalgas* taking the cool summer air.

And I think I was jealous. And I think I was grateful when Coach said that we were the best dudes to come out of Holmes playground. José and I cracked up and hid our grins behind our hands.

We stayed until dusk, and then we finally got a bite worth our attention.

"Be cool, little one," José yelled happily as he got to his feet and worked his pole. He reeled in a blue-gill that was good-sized, one that could feed a family of three or four cats. Or you could fry it and serve it filleted with a bowl of white rice, Japanese style. Which is what José planned for his *abuelo*, his grandfather, who loved fish more than beans and tortillas. For a Mexican, he was a strange one.

We drove back to town, the windshield gathering more bugs. We drove with the radio off and each of us lost in our lazy thoughts. As for me, my thoughts were about Angel. I wanted to tell Coach what I had heard about Angel killing Jesús. I wanted to ask if Angel was that crazy. I had seen him in his share of fights and knew he could hurt people. Still, to stick another, especially a friend, was beyond right or wrong. What lodged in his heart to cause him to do such things? If he had a heart.

We stopped at a drive-in dairy and bought bottles of chocolate milk. We each got our own bottle, nearly as cold as the river. We drank them leaning on a fence, our bellies filling with that beautiful childhood liquid. In the dusk, in that quiet before actual night, cows chewed their grass and the flies chewed their cows.

CHAPTER 8

In bed that night, with the moist summer air sitting on me like a fat bully, I heard footsteps on my porch and the words "Hey, Eddie." Breeze? Creak in the floor? The sound of the plumbing in the walls? Paranoid madness? I jumped out of bed and reached for my home-run bat. I was scared, I admit, but I was ready to drop Angel. I tiptoed into the living room, all the while trying to pick up the source of "Hey, Eddie." My eyes fell shut as I listened for sounds. I heard my neighbor's toilet flush, the clang of the wind chimes in the adjoining yard, and my heart and its good old thump of blood.

I returned to the bed still dented with the shape of my body. Was I going *loco*? Perhaps it was a cat or one of my cockroaches out there taking in the night air. Perhaps it was a stray dog squirting its juice on the already dead plants outside my apartment. *¿Quién sabe?* Who knows? God was snoring on the job. He was letting Angel, the *cholo* made in His own image, run around Fresno.

Toward morning I fell asleep and I woke about ten, groggy. I got up, washed, made coffee, and ate cereal with the TV on. A game show was on and everyone seemed excited about being awake.

"You ain't that happy," I snarled at the television.

The contestants kept jumping up and down, excited that they had won a boat and a freezer full of Grade-A meat for a year.

I hated the winners but kept watching until I eyed a letter in my mail slot. I fetched it quickly. It was from Mom! When I tore it open, I discovered not twenty dollars but three fives, none of them very clean. She would blame the slip on her poor memory or the phone connection at my aunt's house. Maybe she would argue that she had in fact sent twenty, not fifteen, as I had asked. With her hearing aid off, she would cry and call me a liar. What could you do with family? Maybe it was better that my father was dead and I was an only child. I had cartwheeled into manhood. Wow, now look at me. On my own for six months and rooming with cockroaches. And with the telephone dead, no one was calling.

Mom had written a note: She was in Sacramento visiting a friend who was having surgery on her toe and needed help. She said that if I wanted to call Norma, the girl that she and my aunt wanted to set me up with, here was her number.

I pocketed the money but crumpled the note. I dressed and decided to go to the store for more milk, Cocoa Puffs cereal, pinto beans, flour tortillas—whatever I could ring up for fifteen bucks. I left the apartment, cautiously walking up the driveway. On the front lawn I searched the street before I risked strolling into the open. There were a couple of young gangsters playing in the sprinklers with their floppy-legged puppy. Across the street, *viejos* were on a couch, crowing. A leaf blower was howling, but the gardener,

Mexican probably, was out of sight. I didn't like noises that could cover up gunfire. Especially if the gunfire was leveled at me. Nervous, I went back to my apartment steps and sat there with my left knee pumping up and down until the blower stopped. Then I sprang up and started off.

"Hey, Eddie!"

I jumped.

It was Belinda, Junior's wife. She was pushing a stroller up the street.

"I saw your name in the paper." Her mouth was dark red and her hair stiff with whatever spray makes a homegirl hard. "How come they didn't put your picture in?"

Stupid question. No wonder the tattooed tears fell eternally from that beautiful face.

"That's 'cause I didn't have any good clothes."

"You look OK to me."

Pregnant, and she was hitting on me? Junior was locked down in Vacaville, but if he found out that I was with his wife, even just talking to her while she rocked the stroller back and forth, quieting the little gangster swaddled in a blue blanket, he would arrange for his *carnales* to beat me good.

"When Junior messed up, they put his picture in the paper."

"Well, you know," I said. "He was carrying a gun and I didn't have nothing on me." I swallowed. I added, "José is doing pretty good. We went fishing and he caught himself something." Lame talk, I admit, but I kept going because Belinda's mouth was red as fruit. Still, I hesitated to make a move, though she wanted something other than walking her baby up and down the street. It would have caused a lot of trouble. I told her that I was off to get some grub at the store, when, over her shoulder, I spotted Angel at the end of the block. He was standing alone, wearing sawed-off Dickies.

"I got to go, girl," I said to Belinda, skipping backward but keeping Angel in sight. I was waiting for his hand to come up from his waist holding my aunt's gun. Angel could foolishly start blasting from that distance and with Belinda's back to him, he might bring her down. Then Junior would blame me and there would be no way out of that major-league problem.

"Eddie, I got something to tell you," she yelled at me.

There was no time for *chisme.* I turned and cut across the street through a sprinkler. I made it into an alley, and only after I ran its length did I look back and slow to a trot. Angel wasn't at the other end. Instead, there was heat shimmering off the black asphalt. I stopped to catch my breath near a huge cardboard box that had once contained a Westinghouse air conditioner, a 1,200 Btu unit. I had to laugh. I had gone to college for two semesters to study air-conditioning and here I was putting my knowledge to use by identifying the cardboard wrapping I was hiding behind.

I sat there exhausted, sweat crawling over my face like ants. I had run from the police a couple of times and from all sorts of *cholitos* in junior high. I had run from teachers, angry neighbors, and even my mom when her temper flared, a flick of her dish towel burning my butt. I was a regular Speedy Gonzalez, but so tired. I wanted to sit still, to keep from always running.

"What are you doing?" a kid's voice asked.

I scrambled to my feet, spooked.

A kid, two years out of his diapers, possibly older, was leaning over his backyard fence, his baby face half lost in the foliage of an overgrown tree. He was chewing on an apricot.

"Don't scare me like that!" I snapped.

In Fresno, people were always popping up out of nowhere, friends and enemies, aunts and grandparents, and little kids like this eating fruit and taking in the messed-up world from their backyard fences. The kid blinked his long eyelashes at me. He sized me up, and almost correctly, too, because he asked if I was homeless like the people on television.

"What are you talking about?"

He explained he'd seen a program on television about people who had no place to stay. He offered me an apricot, which he tossed down, and repeated, "You got a home?"

I rolled it in my palm and answered, "*Órale*, little man. I got a nine-bedroom house on the bluffs. It's even got a swimming pool."

"How come you're sitting in the dirt?"

There was no answer for that, only a mild chuckle. I didn't have time for this future social worker. Biting into the apricot, I hustled away, uncertain where to go. But I kept sliding, alley after stinky alley, block after desolate block, until I was on Tulare Street in sight of Holmes playground, where I stopped and watched the usual scene: a couple of homies in the parking lot flicking matches at each other, laughing and slapping their arms when the matches hit. What a game, I thought, for these pint-size glue sniffers. I had played the same game when I was their age, and now look at me, I'm all burned up.

I could have gone to see Coach but decided against it, opting to visit Angel instead. I had an appointment to mess him up before he got me, a sort of Golden Rule for homies. My hands were ready, and I had been in so many fights another wouldn't mean much. I had to act first, not second, act so quickly that Angel would go down before he pulled a gun or knife on me.

I bought a soda and two Baby Ruths from a liquor store with mirrors to spot shoplifting placed in every brightly lit corner. I considered reading comics, but there was a sign that said NO BROWSING, MY FRIEND. I left. I ate and drank my kiddie meal as I walked toward Angel's house, looking left, right, behind me, always checking, a permanent flinch in my shoulder. No telling when Angel might rise from behind a parked car and hurt me, cripple me from the waist down, make me regret that I was living.

With my T-shirt tied around my waist, I walked a mile down Tulare Street toward Cedar Avenue, walked past used-car lots, radiator shops, tire shops, and restaurants with their glass doors pressed with fingerprints. There was a Laundromat, empty it seemed, and a boarded-up plumbing shop I remembered stealing a roll of duct tape from when I was eleven. A couple of winos tried to hit on me, and a skinny *ruca* on methadone. I opened my palms up, the gesture of I ain't got nothing, bro.

As I cruised past the A & W Root Beer, I caught

myself in the glare of the window. I combed my hair
with my fingers and flexed my stomach. I figured if
I'm going to die, why should I have to do it on an
empty stomach? The soda and Baby Ruths hadn't
helped much. I put my T-shirt back on and pulled
open the dirty door, letting in flies and the afternoon
heat.

"Be right with you," a girl's voice called from the
kitchen. Her eyes peered from behind the soda machine. "Hey, Eddie!"

It was a girl I knew from high school, and, like
Norma at the City College cafeteria, another success
story selling lunch. I tried to sound happy. I yelled,
"Hi there, girl!"

"You don't remember my name, do you?" she said
as she emerged from the back, wiping her wet hands
on her apron, which was streaked with ketchup. There
was a tomato slice pasted to her apron, too. I wasn't
sure if I should point it out or not, like when you see
a guy's food lodged between his teeth. I let it go.

She anticipated my answer, her smile as big as an
open mailbox. I took a stab. "Lupita!"

"That's right!" She clapped her hands like a con-
testant on a television game show. "We were in pho-
tography together."

I nodded, trying to keep my eyes big with excite-
ment. And they stayed that way because the tomato
slice on her apron fell off.

"Yeah, Lupita," I crowed. Lupita. Waitressing and
cashier work is what you do if you got that name.

"I read about you in the paper," she said. She was
scooping ice from a bin, her smile still on me. "You
didn't get hurt?"

"Nah, just José." I nodded my head. I'm famous, I concluded. If she'd had the clipping from the newspaper, I would have autographed it for her.

She shoved a mug of root beer at me. "Here, it's on me. What else you want?"

The question was open, suggestive. I licked my lips and, examining her throat, ordered a cheeseburger with small fries. The fry cook in the back was already busy, anticipating my order because he could see that I was a meat eater. I snagged a wobbly table near the window that faced Tulare Street—torn-up cars drove by on the torn-up street. This was my *barrio*, the landscape I had known all my life. I had gotten in fights on this street and cut lawns for a *vieja* who had long been gone. I even knew who laid down the CON SAFOS on the wall of the radiator shop. That was Hector Medina, roommate now, for all I knew, with Junior in Vacaville.

I sat up when I spotted Samuel with his two homies walking on the other side of the street. They were kicking around for someone to hurt or something to steal, or both. They walked past, Samuel in the lead, and disappeared from view. He stayed in my mind, though. In my imagination, I was kicking his ass, something he needed more than I needed the poor cheeseburger that was coming my way.

"Punks," I said under my breath. I smiled when Lupita put down my plastic basket of food.

I ate under a fan, which stirred the vapor of greasy smells throughout the restaurant. I was wiping my mouth when a shiver moved my shoulders.

"Belinda," I whispered to myself. I smelled out her *movida* as I pictured her and me rapping in front of my apartment. Angel, fearless dog, had gotten her to hold me there while he snuck up. It was possible. No, it was likely. And it was even more likely that someone would whisper into Junior's ear in Vacaville and then some real war would start. I crushed my napkin and looked up when some jughead workers came into the restaurant. I got up and called, "I'll see you around, Lupita."

Lupita waved with the tips of her fingernails, also bloodred. She hesitated but yelled from the back. "Come and see me! You know where I live."

I left the A & W, swinging the door wide enough for a couple of flies to go in. Even they had to make a living.

Angel's house was dusty white and blooming with flowers, mostly roses. I could smell them from across the street. There was a plum tree, its branches heavy with fruit, and a Chevy Impala smothered in dust from being parked with its engine pulled out. The swamp cooler was squeaking, so I knew someone was home. I watched the house. His parents were probably at work and there was no barking dog on the front porch. I figured that he was alone. I hoped so, because if not, I was in trouble.

I studied that house, the neighborhood. A couple of kids were spraying each other with garden hoses in one front yard. It looked like fun. But it was no fun when a car cruised past and its driver, a *pelón* homie, stared at me. I held the stare until he turned his head like he was looking for traffic. He left me alone, maybe guessing that I was crazy, or if not crazy, then mean enough to pull him from his ride and spank his bald head for looking at me.

I tripped into the alley that was like the alley of every poor neighborhood in Fresno. It stank. Crouched down, I waited fifteen, twenty minutes, maybe longer, in the shade of a fence, and then climbed over the fence into Angel's yard, which, like any other Mexican yard, had a little garden with tomatoes, chiles, eggplant, and tall, rustling corn. There was a stack of bricks and boards, two lawn mowers, both broken, and an old mutt that settled his gaze on me, someone insane enough to jump into *his* yard. His tail went stiff. He ambled heavily toward me as he barked, each time louder. I clicked my fingers to cool him down, whispering, "Hey dude, come on, boy." Maybe because I looked like Angel, brown as dirt, or like one of Angel's friends, the dog stopped barking. Or maybe it was just the afternoon heat and a feeling of why bother with these *vatos*. In any case, the dog didn't want to get involved.

I hid before the back door opened and Angel's voice screamed to the dog, "Shut up, Humo, or I'm gonna beat your ass!" The dog whined and started toward the door for a soothing pat on the head, but the door closed with a sigh. That was Angel, one nice dude.

I hunkered in the family garden and squeezed a tomato. The seeds rolled out like teeth and the juice like blood. Flies buzzed me. Gnats hung around my ears.

"Get away," I muttered at these insects.

I waited another ten minutes and even petted the dog, whispering, "Humo, you're a cool dog." But finally I made my move. I scrambled closer to the kitchen door. Sweat poured from me, and my chest rose and fell. I had to get Angel. I settled into a crouching position on the side of the house, just out of view of the kitchen door. I threw a trowel at the dog, then a baseball mitt that was stiff from lying discarded in the rain and sun. The dog started yapping again.

Come out, Angel, I begged. Both fists were closed, then open, then closed again. I was pumping myself up with fury.

I dug up a potted plant and tossed it, not meanly, just accurately, at Humo. The plant landed on the dog's back and stayed there. Humo pranced in circles, baffled by what was on his back. I almost laughed, and I would have except I heard footsteps pounding toward the back door. I was ready. When the door opened, I leapt and grabbed Angel by the legs, so that he fell backward and hit his head against the doorjamb. I pummeled him with a two-fisted action as he scratched like a little girl and kicked his legs free. I let him up and got off a clean hit to his jaw. He fell into a sitting position and I jumped on him again. We rolled in the doorway.

"You killed Jesús, you mother," I screamed into his bloody face.

"What kinda shit are you talking, homes?" His hand crawled toward my throat.

I elbowed him in his ear and he cried from the pain.

"You killed my *primo*! You said some guy in yellow shoes did it! That's bullshit, man!" I was exhausted, shaking. Fire ate up the good air in my lungs. Tears of rage spilled from my eyes.

"I didn't," he cried. His hand was clawing me. It hurt, and I would have borne that hurt except I felt a thump on my back. Two more thumps and I rolled over to face Samuel. Maybe he'd surfaced from hell itself. He raised a stick and I blocked it with my forearms, blocked and grabbed it so that it was mine.

But Angel was up, blood flowing from his nose, and before I could use the stick on Samuel, who was backpedaling with fear on his *cholo* face, Angel kicked me in the ribs. The stick slipped from my hands. I rolled onto my stomach and then my back, rolled like a carpet to keep them from getting me. My breath was gone and I would have been a dead boy on the patio, except they were too cautious. They circled me, Samuel now with the stick and Angel with the pot that held the plant. Each of them thought the other would attack. But they both circled, taunting me.

"I didn't kill Jesús!" Angel yelled.

"You lie, man!"

"I would never hurt a friend." With that, Angel hurled the pot at me and clipped my shoulder.

"You're weak!" I cried at Angel.

Humo was barking at all of us. A dog in the next yard joined him.

"He was my *carnal*!" Angel yelled at me as he leaned against the house. His face was wrinkled from pain. His ear was already bloating up. I hit Angel again and Samuel swung the stick at me. He missed and I got him with a side kick that gushed air from his little-boy lungs. His eyes closed from the pain. The stick dropped from his hand as he bent over, head down. I gripped his head in a headlock, squeezed, and ran and plowed him against the wall of the house, where he collapsed and stayed down. Right there, the *cholito* was learning about the ABC's of gang life.

"Asshole," I cursed at Samuel, but when I turned, Angel had disappeared. He's in the house, I thought. I pictured my auntie's gun wrapped in a dish towel. I pictured Angel staggering back through the kitchen, the gun raised.

I limped to the back fence and hopped over. I limped up the alley and when I got to the end, I looked back. Angel was standing there, alone and small. I turned and limped away, dragging my hard-luck shadow.

José and I sat in his bedroom, with his television on and his radio on, too. I blew my bloody nose into an old gym sock that he had pulled from a drawer. He didn't want it anymore, and I was a dude in need. I examined the blood: It was rich, hot, and to me, a beautiful fluid. My mouth was swollen, my shoulder cut from the pot, and my back ached from Samuel whacking me with that stick. I touched my ribs. A bruise had already appeared and so had another on my left leg. I didn't remember hurting my leg, but the quarter-size bruise and pain were there.

I drank the remainder of my soda, rattling the ice cubes in my glass, which sported the Los Angeles Raiders emblem. I clawed an ice cube and ran it across my swollen lip. I skipped the details, but told José that Angel and I threw nine rounds of *chingasos*. Angel is hurt, I managed to mumble, and Samuel is waking with a headache just about now.

"Did you use the throat chop I taught you?" José asked, the marine still in him.

I shook my head.

"I'll get you another soda," José said as he sprang up from his bed. His macho marine attitude was gone. I was happy to be with him and told him so before he left the room.

"You and me go way back, Eddie," he said.

And we did.

He left his bedroom, and I could hear his mother saying in Spanish that I was bad luck, *mala suerte.* Maybe so. They moved their conversation away from the bedroom, leaving me staring at José's television, his high school graduation present. The sound was down low, but I was aware that happiness existed in the world. The contestants jumped up and down, more winners with boats and Grade-A meat for a year.

José returned with a cream soda and a pile of ice cubes wrapped in a dish towel. I cooled my shoulder, lip, leg, and rib. The rib was the most tender, having taken a direct kick from Angel. On the floor, I lay on my stomach and, grimacing, praying that it wouldn't hurt that much, let José set the dish towel on my bruised back.

"You're all messed up, bro," José said.

There was no way to argue.

José's mother called him in her Mexican singsong voice. She called three more times before he slowly rose to his feet, carefully because of his stitches. "My mom's still mad at you."

I wasn't making too many people happy, and that included myself. "Yeah, I know."

He left the bedroom, quietly closing the door behind him, and I heard them talking in whispers before José's voice rose in anger. He told her that I was his friend and she wasn't going to do anything to embarrass me. I assumed she wanted to throw me out of the house.

He returned to the bedroom, a moody cloud floating across his face. He didn't say anything, and I didn't ask.

I told José that I was sorry that I ruined his sock and he said, "Don't worry, homes. I got a whole drawer of them!"

José journeyed inside himself, cloud after stormy cloud passing over his face. He said that we lived in a hellhole and there was no way out. "Even if you try to do something, people mess you up." He yakked fifteen minutes straight without my stopping him.

I cooled my body with ice cubes. At about four o'clock he asked if I wanted to go with him to the hospital. The stitches in his shoulder had to come out.

"Yeah, sounds good," I mumbled. I slowly rose to my feet and realized how sore I was. In his bathroom, I examined my face, a cut above the brow and a swollen lower lip. My left eye was flecked with blood.

I washed my face. In the living room, I blurted to José's mother that I was sorry José got messed up on account of me.

I think she was shocked at my wounds.

"Where's your mother?" she asked in Spanish. She tried to straighten up the neck of my stretched-out T-shirt.

I shrugged.

José had a clean T-shirt for me with a Fresno State bulldog on the front. We left in his mother's car, an ancient Impala with two mismatched fenders. His moodiness evaporated in the afternoon heat. He adjusted the rearview mirror but the mirror fell. The heat made everything wilt.

"Damn thing," he growled.

Maybe there was no way to look back. Maybe we should stare into the future. I didn't even try to help with the rearview mirror.

We drove with the radio off because there was nothing to sing about as far as we could tell, both of us all banged up. I sat with my hands in my lap, eyes straight ahead. We drove down Tulare Street, right past the A & W Root Beer.

"Lupita works there," I said weakly.

"Who's Lupita?"

"I don't know. Just a girl."

Bumpy Tulare Street with its potholes the size of dry ponds made more blood flow from my nose, not a lot but enough for its salty taste to slither down my throat.

"You OK, Eddie?" José asked. He had rested his hand on my arm.

"Couldn't be better." I smiled. I dabbed my nose. I gazed down at the blood-flecked front of José's T-shirt.

"José," I said, "I ruined your T-shirt."

"That's OK."

At the hospital, we rode the elevator to the second floor to station two, where they put in and ripped out stitches and gave old folks injections during flu season. The place was busy with babies who tripped and knocked their heads, and grandpas who did the same. There were gangsters, too. I eyed one *cholo* in a hair net and he eyed me, too, but we were both too weak to bother with a stare down.

José checked in and we sat down in orange plastic chairs. I picked up a *People* magazine, thumbed it once, and slapped it against my knee. I was nervous. I didn't like this place. I remembered the hospital entrance with more people going in than leaving. Luckily, we didn't wait long. José was called over a loudspeaker. "You want to wait," he asked, "or come with me?"

"I'll go. I want to see how they do it."

I put down my magazine and followed José through the swinging door. The Filipino nurse met us. She asked, "Which one of you is José?"

José pointed to himself.

"Then you go have a seat," she told me. She winced at the blood on the front of my bulldog T-shirt.

"Can't," I said. "My friend can't speak English."

José smiled, willing to play along. He said loudly, "No speak." He jabbed me in the shoulder roughly. "Me friend."

The nurse led us down a hallway yellow as Oz's brick road. We thought we were headed to a private room, but no such luck. In a large room filled with screaming babies and kids, the nurse instructed José to sit down and wait his turn. A boy about ten was getting stitches taken out of his brow and another kid, towel pressed to his chin, was kicking his legs back and forth, back and forth. He knew he was next, the little champ, and he was ready. The place was a real factory, stitches going in and coming out.

"Remember," I whispered. "You can't speak English."

"I know that," José said. "I got C's in it all my life!"

We laughed. Then José's name was called and an RN picked up his chart, calling him a second time, this time louder and not playing with us.

"Come on, young man," the nurse commanded. She was wearing gloves. For a joke, I brought out my bloody gym sock, and when she saw it she recoiled.

"Are you hurt?" she asked.

I sniffed up my bloody *mocos*. I blew my nose. "Nah, I'm feeling pretty good."

"Go sit down!"

"My friend here don't speak English good."

"Go sit down—now!"

I did what I was told and before I knew it, José had his shirt off and the nurse was plucking at his stitches with tweezers. José twisted his head and grinned at me. He gave me a thumbs-up sign. He was out in ten minutes, like a lube and oil change.

We were out of there, José rotating his arm and saying that he felt pretty good but that there was still a little stiffness.

"Let me see, man," I asked as I limped along beside him.

"Not here." He pushed me away when I tried to take a peek. Right before my eyes José was getting better. I was, too. My nose had stopped bleeding.

Instead of taking the elevator we took the stairs, and whether it was God's choice or the devil's I don't know, but at the landing at the bottom stood Angel, his eye swollen from a row of new stitches. He was climbing the steps but stopped when he saw me. We looked at each other for a moment, as if we weren't sure where we had seen each other before. We stared as if we were cousins or distant relatives. Then his eyes blazed, and before he could reach under his T-shirt, I raced down the steps, nearly tripping, blood already flowing from my nose, and I was on him. I cursed him and he cursed me. The sick, the relatives of the sick, hospital workers, at least two nurses, all scattered as we rolled over each other down a narrow flight of stairs.

CHAPTER 9

Maybe the mortuary students will get extra credit for washing the tattooed bodies of us *cholos* who can't afford a regular paid-for burial. Maybe they will tie our ties, button down our collars, rub a little pink into our cheeks, and then, with a heave-ho, lift our bodies into out-of-style coffins. The way we tore into each other, tumbling down the stairway and throwing *chingasos* at the landing, the mortuary students almost got to carry Angel and me away. Instead, security was called, two old Filipinos in polyester suits too big for them. When they saw us, they gave us room, jabbering in their island language, and backed away.

Angel and I were smart enough to scramble away from the hospital, both of us bleeding a trail as ancient as the first *pachucos* of the 1940s. When you see a homie staggering up the street, you give him room. You move to the other side of the sidewalk, whistling "Dixie"—or "Cielito Lindo" in our case.

José pulled up next to me in his mother's car, but I waved him off. He was crying, this marine who, without even leaving his country, had seen enough wars to be permanently scarred. He begged me over and over to get in. His car kept pace with my staggering, but I ignored him. I turned my face toward his, twisted with sobbing. The rearview mirror was still wilted. It was hanging like my head. I tried to say, "Fix your mirror, man," but I couldn't talk. I waved him off. His car stopped in the street and I stumbled on, cutting across a vacant lot, my socks picking up foxtails and dirt.

I limped toward my apartment, and in a lawn sprinkler I washed my face, neck, and arms. I stripped off José's bulldog T-shirt and let the spray hit my chest. I rested twice, both times in alleys, and once came across a couple of homies sitting on a car fender. They were curious, but that's all. They let me pass.

That night, with no help from the mortuary students, I soaked myself in the bathtub and washed my body with a tenderness that amazed me. There was nothing to be done with my face: My left eye was closed and my mouth was so swollen that I couldn't form words. My nose was large. My scalp hurt, and my throat was savagely red. What had I done to myself? I put ice cubes on my wounds, but still the heat from the bruises didn't let up.

Lupe showed up that night, screaming like a fool. While he didn't have anything really against me, he was mad at me for smashing Samuel's head into the wall. He called me a bunch of names and told me to come out because he wanted to kick my ass. I couldn't speak. I lay on the living-room floor in a dark corner, eye level with a couple of cockroaches. He pressed his face in every window, but I was out of sight. He called my mother names. He punched his fist into one of the windows and glass flew into the room. He stuck his head through the jagged window, an animal looking in. But the noise drew out my neighbor, Mrs. Rios, who lived in the front duplex, and she scolded him for being a troublemaker. Lupe trotted away, but not before he yelled a litany of exaggerated threats. No way was he going to kill me nine times. Once would do it.

Mrs. Rios knocked on my door, cooed nice words, and asked in Spanish, then English, if I was OK. I mumbled through the door, "*Sí*. I'm sleepy." That was all I could manage. She stayed on my porch, listening for a moment. Then she shuffled back to her own apartment. I heard her porch light snap on.

As I lay on the floor, I thought about my cousin Jesús's stabbing. Maybe Angel hadn't killed him after all. Maybe it was *chisme*, just something for Norma to say while she kicked her legs in her swimming pool. Maybe Norma really thought that Angel had killed Jesús because she had picked up the rumor from a homegirl. In Fresno, with nothing to do, people spread rumors like everything, and before you knew it, you were the topic. I lay on the floor and pictured a dude in yellow shoes. He was kicking me, and not lightly, either. I fell asleep to this thrashing.

Two days later, with a cardboard carton of clothes and a half-empty cereal box in my arms, I walked the three miles to my *nina*'s house. She cried when she saw me, cried because of the beating I had taken and because I was the last one to see Queenie alive. She told me that. She offered me a soda and leftover Campbell's soup, which I sipped carefully at her kitchen table. The soup was good, and the soda was as cool as a river. I told her through my swollen mouth that I had given her dog a nice hug before I let her go.

Two weeks later my *nina* dropped me off at the

naval recruiting office and gave me a hug that squeezed the hurt inside me. I had to get out of town, and signing up was the only way. I didn't tell Coach or José. They both thought I had gone to spend time with my mom in Merced. Not a chance. When I called my mom from my *nina*'s house, my bruises had healed. I figured that Angel would be healing at the same time and would soon be after me. He had my aunt's gun and the next time he would use it. I had to leave. It was July, really hot, with a fiery sun holding us down.

My *nina* hugged me and pressed ten dollars into my palm, which I wanted to press back into her hand. I didn't deserve it. I was the lowlife who'd snagged her money when Queenie gave up the ghost.

My mother didn't see me off, but she sent a letter saying how much she loved me, plus fifteen dollars.

My *nina* drove away from the recruiting office with both hands on the wheel. I felt like crying. All my life everyone was pulling away from me—Father, my mom, Jesús, school friends, and homies who disappeared in three lines of the obituary column. I could have cried under the heat of Fresno, but it wouldn't have mattered. My tears would have evaporated before anyone saw my sadness. I picked up my two suitcases and pushed open the door of the recruiting office with a kick of my shoe. The coolness felt good. Some dudes in chairs raised their faces to me. If I hadn't been holding the suitcases, I would have beat my palm against my forehead. Larry the stoner was one of them. He grinned and yelled, "Eddie! We're in together." Look at the company I keep, I thought. It's either homies or stoners.

"They got free sodas!" he yelled as he helped me with a suitcase. He pulled my arm to show me an ice chest. That was our welcome—free Safeway-brand sodas floating in cloudy water.

At two o'clock we boarded a small van for the drive to Lemoore Naval Air Station, a hundred miles southwest of Fresno, in the desert, where the heat was even more vicious. Funny, I thought. We're joining the navy, but the navy is in the desert. I just hoped that what José told me about the service was true: all the chocolate milk you could drink. I hoped that the navy could teach me to swim like a dolphin and fight like a crocodile.

A not particularly clean van shoved off with us new recruits, one who was teary-eyed leaving his girlfriend and another who was laughing about escaping a girlfriend with mean redneck brothers. Right away, these two didn't get along. I kept to myself, while Larry sat near the driver. They were talking about Guns N' Roses.

We roared onto Highway 99 then took the 41 junction, escaping the city into farmland. We sped by mile after mile of grape and cotton fields. The highway was littered with roadkill—dogs, and a few chickens with their legs in the air. There were junkyards, too, and gas stations. But the farther we drove, the fewer people we saw. Just farms and farm animals.

Near Riverdale, the van started to overheat. Steam clouded the windshield. The engine knocked and groaned, and in no time we were on the side of a small two-lane highway.

One by one we piled out of the van onto the crunch of gravel. At first the heat wasn't fierce. The sun was just bright, so that we had to squint as we complained good-naturedly. The driver threw open the hood of the van. He didn't know what to do, and we didn't know, either, except to cuss and immediately snag the last of the free sodas. As we drank the sodas, a car whizzed by, heavy on the horn. The passenger threw a bottle at us and every one of us badass new recruits stabbed the finger at the car.

The heat pressed us into the shadow of the van as we waited for the CHP. Two of the dudes took off their shirts and tossed them on their heads. Larry the stoner did the same. I was surprised that he had a couple of wounds, knife scars, on a pale body. All of us could have taken off our shirts and shown our wounds, each pink and velvety to the touch. When they started talking about girls, braggart stories that were untrue and biologically impossible, I walked away over the gravel toward a car that was about a half-mile up the road. It was shining in the middle of the field, abandoned maybe. I crossed the highway when traffic was slow. Now and then a huge diesel growled down the highway, and cars with trailers. But it was mostly quiet. The black birds on the barbed wire squawked. A rabbit kicked up dirt in the fields.

I walked toward the car and hopped a barbed-wire fence into the field, where huge, landlocked seagulls were picking at the earth. I didn't know the crop, but whatever it was had already been harvested. My attention was on two men, both black, both in tattered clothes, who were gathering what was left after the harvest. I hesitated in the field, hesitated because what were these men but miracles?

"No, it can't be!" I cried to myself as I hurried

toward them. Their shirts were unbuttoned and whipping about them. I hurried over the clods, my legs suddenly heavy, hurried to meet these brothers. I slowed to a stop. I stood within a yard of them and could have touched their faces but knew it wouldn't be right. They were dirty but hard-muscled, these men who were sweaty but making a living from leftovers.

"Hey, man, I seen you before." One of them grinned, the one from Cuca's restaurant.

My god, I thought. My wounds hurt, my lungs were on fire. I was overwhelmed with sorrow. I realized I had trudged over onions, acres of buried onions.

"Where I seen you before, my friend?" the man asked. He raked a large hand across his brow.

"I don't know," I sobbed. I turned to look back at the van, which seemed so far away that I could never get back.

"I sell you some, huh? They good, huh?"

I hunched down, my hands to my face to hide the shame that had brought me to this field. I saw Jesús on the ground, then Angel over him. I saw my palms bloodred from all the city wars—those in the past, those now, and those to come when every homie would raise a fist to his brother. Without saying a word, the man raised me up and handed me onions, one for each hand. And whether it was from the sun or the whipping wind, my eyes filled and then closed on the last of childhood tears.

SPANISH WORDS
AND PHRASES

abrazo	hug
abuelita	little "dear" grandma
abuelo	grandfather
¡Ándale!	Hurry up! or Let's go!
¡Ay, Dios!	Oh, God!
beso	kiss
bravo	brave
burro	donkey
cabrón	bastard
carnal	blood brother
carnales	blood sisters
¡Chale!	No way!
chango	monkey
chingaso	fight, throwing a blow
chisme	rumor, gossip
chola	girl (possibly gang girl)
cholo	boy (possibly gang boy)
chones	underwear
cochino	dirty
comadre	dear female friend
Con Safos	graffiti sign-off term, as in Amen
de veras	really
diablito	little devil
¿Entiendes?	Do you understand?

147

flaco	skinny (or skinny boy)
fuchi	smelly
gavacho	white person
gordito	chubby (or chubby boy)
helado	ice cream
hombre a hombre	man to man
la señora	the lady; Mrs.
loco	crazy
mala suerte	bad luck
mallate	black person
maraca	rattling percussion intrument made from a gourd
mentiroso	liar
mi'jo	my son; my dear
¡Míra!	Look!
mocos	mucus
mocoso	little snot (as in a kid is a little snot)
movida	secret plan; move
nalgas	butt
nina	godmother
Órale!	Hey! or Alright!
pachuco	zoot-suiter
paleta	ice-cream bar
pan dulce	sweet bread
pantalones	pants
papas	potatoes
pelón	bald
pinche	rascal
pinto	prisoner
placa	name, mostly on walls
pobrecita	poor thing; poor girl
primo	cousin

puro malo	only bad
¿Quién sabe?	Who knows?
raspada	snow cone
ratoncito	little rat
raza	race
ruca	girl (derogatory)
suave	mellow
Tejano	Texan man
telenovela	soap opera
tía	aunt
tonto	stupid
travieso	mischevious, naughty person
vato	dude
vendedora	saleswoman
vieja	old; old woman
viejo	old; old man
¿Y qué?	And so what?

READER CHAT PAGE

1. Why does Eddie ignore all of *Tía* Dolores's pleas for him to avenge Jesús's death? Why does *Tía* Dolores think he can get away with murder?

2. Eddie recalls how he used to hang out with Angel and his crew, but he tries to stay away now. Have you ever made an effort to change your behavior? How are you different now than you were two years ago?

3. How does Coach help Eddie? Is there an adult in your life, aside from a parent, whom you could turn to for help and advice the way Eddie turns to Coach?

4. What did you think of how Eddie dealt with the theft and eventual recovery of Mr. Stiles's truck? What might have happened if he had called the police?

5. Do you think Mr. Stiles was right to set Eddie up? What would you have done if you were in Mr. Stiles's position?

6. Do you think Eddie was wrong to pocket some of the money his *nina* gave him to donate to the SPCA? Why or why not?

7. How is José different from Angel? How might Angel have reacted if he had been there when Eddie saw Mr. Stiles's truck? How might José have reacted if *Tía* Dolores asked him to avenge the death of Jesús?

8. Why does Eddie join the navy? How does he feel about his decision? What are his other options?